Their Merry Little Christmas

A Love Square Holiday Novella

Jessica Ingro

THEIR MERRY LITTLE CHRISTMAS

Copyright © 2013 by Jessica Ingro

Cover design © Arijana Karčić, Cover It! Designs
Edited by Kathy Krick

ISBN: 1494345854
ISBN-13: 978-1494345853

To my naughty girls… this is for you!

Acknowledgements

To my husband and family – I couldn't do this without you! Lots of love for you!

Debi Barnes – you are my better half! What you do for me is invaluable and you'll never be able to shake me.. So don't even try. Next up is Elizabeth & Grant! Finally!

Elle Wilson – thank you for teaching me the French language! I will continue to creepily read your mind and make you type an inordinate amount of inappropriate comments. Your penis face shirt is in the mail!

Alicia Clark – you will need to fight me for Jacob! Thanks for your insight!

Ari Karčić – you knocked this one out of the park! Here's to many more!

Kathy Krick – Thanks again doll for rockin' with me and the Love Square gang!

To all the bloggers I've had the pleasure of interacting with… Thank you!

And to Jennifer at Love Between the Sheets, Lisa & Jennifer from Three Chicks & Their Books, and Emily at the SubClub Books… A huge thank you for your support and kindness. I owe you guys one… or maybe a few!

And for the rest of you… Thank you! Have yourself a merry little Christmas!

Table of Contents

Sam

"You better watch out. You better not cry…" I sing along loudly to the radio as I push little Hershey Kisses into the top of each peanut butter cookie. I smirk thinking of the name my grandfather always called them: "Itty Bitty Titties." My crazy grandfather. I shake my head and refuse to let the sadness of his death overtake Christmas cookie making. Only the good memories are allowed to consume me.

"Santa Claus is coming to town…" I reach down and grab Tessa off the floor, where she is playing with her LaLaLoopsie doll, and twirl her around. Her little laugh is infectious as I continue singing to her.

"Wuv you, mommy," my sweet daughter says and gives me a hug. I cherish moments like this.

"Love you too, baby," I whisper and squeeze her tighter.

"Mommy has such a pretty voice, doesn't she Tessa?" Aiden says from the doorway to the kitchen. There is a grin on his face, and it looks like he is biting back laughter.

Yeah, yeah. Laugh away Aiden. Your singing voice isn't much better.

"Will you can it? I'm not in the mood to be made fun of. I'm enjoying myself and don't want you to ruin it." I set Tessa down to play with her doll.

"Sorry, honey. You know I can't help myself. I love teasing you." He kisses my neck behind my ear and sends shivers down my spine. The bastard knows what he's doing. Kissing me there is the easiest way to turn me on.

Two can play this game…

"Are all these cookies for the ladies at my office?" Aiden asks before popping a chocolate filled cookie in his mouth.

"Yes. And don't eat those." I slap his hand playfully and laugh when he groans.

"Why can't I eat any? You can't tempt a man this way. It's not right," he grumbles good naturedly.

"I can do anything I please. Besides, I'm making some cookies for our friends and family too. There will be plenty for you to eat once I divvy them all out."

The timer on the oven sounds and I mentally smile at what I'm about to do next. I grab a pot holder and bend over at the waist, giving my derriere a little shake, knowing full well Aiden is watching me.

Men… so predictable.

I take my time and set the cookie sheets on the stove top. I rise slowly, swinging my hair back – ala a 1980's rock video. My head turns and I watch Aiden's throat work as he swallows. Ha ha. Sam – one; Aiden – zero.

"So not fair," he mutters before grabbing another cookie and popping it in his mouth.

"The 'Elf on a Shelf' set finally got delivered today. I'm so excited to get it out and start playing with it." I pick up the conversation, deciding to ignore the fact that he ate yet another cookie.

"You have real issues, you know that right? Tessa isn't quite two years old yet and you're going crazy with presents and decorations. I thought I had at least another year before your obsessive personality kicked in for this stuff," Aiden complains.

"Look. It's important to me. That's all you need to know... And understand." I add for good measure.

"Just don't run yourself ragged doing this. It's not the most important thing. Okay?"

I nod my head and mumble in agreement under my breath, continuing to set the warm cookies on the cooling racks.

"Daddy? Wanna watch Elmo," Tessa says while tugging on Aiden's pant leg to get his attention.

"Sure thing, Babygirl." He scoops her up in his arms and walks over to me.

"We'll finish this later," he whispers his promise and kisses my nose. I smile, knowing how much fun it will be to finish our game later. Having a child puts a damper on your sexual spontaneity, but I must say the anticipation of being alone after she is asleep certainly makes it worth it.

I turn up the radio now that Tessa is with Aiden and continue working on the cookies. Baking has become a way for me to chill out. I enjoy making treats and goodies. And while I try not to sample my goods too much, I have to admit I've gained a pound or two since I really got into this.

Last Christmas we hired an assistant for me. Her name is Lily, and she is my godsend. She handles all my social media accounts, and she interacts with my street team and bloggers. Gone are the days of worrying about giveaways and deadlines. That is what she's for. She keeps me moving and on target. Thanks to her I have time to do things I want to do, like baking.

I love her like she was a niece. She is young – barely twenty-one – and has no family nearby. Aiden and I have taken her under our wings. She's even planning on spending some time with us on Christmas when we go to my mother-in-law's. She is such a recluse that I'm hoping I can get her involved with more people and maybe even find a nice boy for her.

Aiden's cell phone buzzes on the counter. I wipe my hands on a towel and pick it up. The screen flashes the name Rocky, and I shrug wondering who Rocky is. I jog into the family room and hand him the phone.

"It's Rocky," I say while he flips it open.

"Hey, Rocky. What's up?" His face looks relaxed and content while he listens to the unknown Rocky. "Yeah sure.

I can meet you over there. It's no problem. I'll be there in a half hour."

"You're leaving?" I ask after he hangs up the phone, trying not to show my discontent that he won't be spending Saturday afternoon with us.

"The Tillman project ran into a few snags this morning. I'm going to go offer some advice. I shouldn't be gone long." He kisses Tessa's head and walks up the stairs to get ready to leave.

Well damn. I thought these weekend excursions were over now that things had died down at work for him. I could really use the help with Tessa while I try to get all this baking done.

I cover Tessa with a blanket and sit next to her on the couch, letting her finish watching her DVD before making her come back in the kitchen with me. When Aiden comes down the stairs, I tip my head on the back of the couch, and he leans over to kiss my mouth.

"Who is Rocky?" I ask before he can leave.

"Just a new architect at work." He shrugs and kisses Tessa's head. "I'll see you in a little while. I'll call if I'm going to be late."

My heart sinks at his last statement. That isn't what I wanted to hear. This Christmas season is really important to me, for more reasons than he knows. I just wish I felt like it was as important to him too.

I shake off my impending bad mood and focus on Elmo. Singing to Tessa and tickling her, quickly helps me to forget that Aiden is missing again.

Jacob

"So what are you getting Kara for Christmas?"

I turn to look at Mack. We've been watching video surveillance for what feels like forever, in an attempt to gather evidence against a murder suspect. I have to shake myself from my stupor. I feel like a zombie after watching hours of people walking in and out of a parking garage.

"A yellow diamond necklace from Tiffany's. She's going to love it." My lips start to turn up into a grin at the thought of how much Kara is going to love the little piece of sunshine I'm giving her. I figure she's given me enough of it over the last couple of years. I owe her some back. I'm thinking this is going to become a recurring theme for my gifts to her. It's perfect really.

Mack raises his eyebrows and whistles. "You can never go wrong with diamonds my man."

"Tell me about it." A yawn escapes me and I shift in my chair, stretching my legs out in front of me. We've been cooped up in here for far too long and have yet to spot the man we're looking for. Finding the bad guys isn't always exciting. In fact, it's rarely like anything you see on television. Yet everyone who has seen those shows expects us to find them swiftly and easily. I hate to break it to the world at large, but DNA tests take far longer than twenty-four hours to come back, and criminals don't always leave behind clues.

Mack looks at his watch and groans. "I'm not sure how much more of this I can take today."

"I couldn't agree with you more. I wouldn't mind getting home at a reasonable time tonight. I haven't gotten to spend quality time with Kara in a few days, if you know what I mean."

He gives me a knowing grin before giving in. "Then let's get one of the interns to keep looking through these and flag anything that looks suspicious. I don't think we're going to find anything anyway. Witness accounts place him in the area an hour earlier than our current spot in this footage. At this point, it's just a precaution."

"Works for me." I clap my hands and stand, stretching my sore muscles. Now that I am headed out of here, my mind starts to wander to what I want to do to Kara tonight. Visions of her naked and writhing in front of the fireplace have my jeans starting to tighten. For as uncomfortable as it is to be in a constant state of arousal, I secretly hope things will always be this way between us. She consistently turns me inside out, and I can't seem to get enough of her.

I follow Mack out of the room, we grab our coats and head out towards the front desk. While he talks to Regina about putting an intern on our assignment, I stand to the side and wait for him. Facing the front door, I spot a familiar face walking in. Just as the previous times I've seen her, her black hair is pulled back into a tight bun low on her head, and her glasses are perched on her nose making her look intellectual and serious. Her blue scrubs peek out from under her heavy coat, telling me she must have come straight from the hospital.

Mack joins me, and his eyes follow mine. His body stiffens slightly, and I'm more than a little curious about his reaction.

"Isn't that Dr. Huntley from Sibley Memorial Hospital?" I ask, nudging Mack with my elbow.

"Yeah. I believe it is."

I watch as his eyes track her movement. She meets up with Detective John Katz and kisses his cheek, before following him back towards the interrogation rooms.

"I wonder what that was all about."

"I'm not sure." He clears his throat before taking a step in that direction. "I'll catch you tomorrow. I have something I need to take care of."

I don't even bother responding because he's quickly gone, following after John and the good doctor. I shake my head, perplexed by his actions.

Chapter Two

Sam

I look at the clock for the umpteenth time and continue seething. What I wouldn't give for a glass of wine to soothe my frayed nerves right about now.

Seeing as how it's eight o'clock, Tessa has long since gone to bed and my husband isn't answering his phone – I think I have the right to be upset. Aiden called to tell me to save him dinner, but that was the last I heard from him. I realize his job is important, but I cannot stand when it comes with a lack of communication. It isn't just him and me anymore.

I finish packaging the last of the Christmas cookies to give away and wrap tin foil around the platters that are staying here. Thankfully, Lily was bored and stopped by today. She watched Tessa while I baked so that I didn't fall behind. Like I said… she's a godsend.

The sound of the garage door grabs my attention. Glancing at the clock, I note that it is now quarter to nine. Aiden has been gone for over seven hours. *Bastard.*

"Sorry, I'm late," he says as soon as he walks through the door.

"Mmm hmmm," I answer, not wanting to talk to him right now.

My body stiffens when he puts his arms around my waist and rests his chin on my shoulder.

"You're mad?" He asks, feeling the tension in my body.

"What do you think?" I snap at him.

"Whoa. That's a little uncalled for, don't you think? I had to go into work. That happens sometimes. You know this," he defends himself.

"I know that you called me four hours ago to say to save you dinner and here it is almost nine o'clock and you traipse in like nothing happened. Your daughter went to bed hours ago. What kind of work could you possibly be doing this late at night?" I turn in his arms and step back from his embrace. I put my hands on my hips in the universal "I'm pissed" gesture.

"I ended up going to dinner with Todd and Rocky after we worked out the design flaws for the contractors. I'm sorry I didn't check in again. Maybe next time you can put a GPS tracker on me," he says sarcastically.

Okay, maybe I do sound a bit ridiculous. It was just one day he bailed on. If it was a reoccurring thing, then I guess I'd have more of a leg to stand on. The wind leaves my sails, and I sag into the counter.

"Sorry. I just... I don't know. I don't like not having you when we should have you. It gets lonely without you sometimes." I shrug and fight the tears that want to come.

Aiden steps towards me and wraps his arms around me, holding me tightly. His warmth seeps into me, and I rest my head on his chest.

"I'm sorry, too. I should have come home. I forget that even though you work, you don't get a lot of adult interaction." His cheek rests on my head, and his hands caress my back.

"I do believe we were due to pick up where we left off. I've been thinking about this all day," he murmurs after several minutes and dips his hand into my pants to cup my ass.

I lift my head, and his mouth lowers down onto mine. Our tongues glide sensuously against each other, and I feel my body temperature rising with the promise of what is to come.

His hand leaves my pants and proceeds to lift my shirt over my head. With one hand, his fingers release my bra. I drop my arms and let it drift to the floor between us. His head dips down and he catches my nipple with his teeth, and then soothes the resulting sting with his tongue. My head drops back, loving the way his tongue flicks against my pebbled nipple, making the throbbing between my legs intensify.

I run my hands under his shirt, up over his smooth, muscular back as he continues to torment my breasts. I grab the hem of his shirt and raise it, making his mouth release my breast in a pop. Before he can attack me again, I drop to my knees. Looking up into his hooded eyes, my fingers open his belt and unbutton his jeans. I push them down his legs. He toes his shoes off and kicks his jeans away, never breaking eye contact.

I reach up and cup his balls, rolling them gently in my hand. My other hand wraps around his long, beautiful cock. My thumb runs along the vein on its underside and over the head. Aiden's breathing picks up and grows louder as I continue caressing his length and teasing him.

"Suck it," his voice is low and gravelly, causing a fresh surge of wetness between my legs.

I replace my thumb with my tongue and run it along the same path I've been tormenting him with. After a few more minutes of torture, his hands lace in my hair and hold my head still. He shifts so his cock rests on my lower lip.

"Suck it," he repeats before pushing into my mouth. I silently accept his length and watch his face contort in pleasure while he moves in and out of my mouth.

"Fuck Sam," he grits out between clenched teeth. "That feels so fucking good."

His hands drop from my head and leave me to work him at my own pace. I relish taking him deep in my throat and swallowing around him. Each time I do, a growl comes from deep in his chest. His enjoyment spurs me into working him faster and sucking a little harder with each pass between my lips.

Needing to relieve the building pressure between my legs, my other hand dips into my pants to find my tight, aching bundle of nerves. I moan when my finger hits its target.

"Shit, I'm not going to last if you don't stop." Aiden curses as he pulls out of my mouth.

His hands go under my armpits, and he raises me off the floor. Once I'm standing, his hands sweep my yoga pants and underwear down my legs. Before they've fully cleared my one foot, he lifts me up on the countertop and spreads my legs wide. His face looks pained as his fingers run along my slit, spreading the wetness around my clit.

I fall back on the counter and close my eyes as the exquisite pleasure builds in my core. Each time his thumb circles my clit and his finger pumps in and out, I want to cry out in pleasure. Just when I'm ready to fall over the edge into sheer and utter bliss, Aiden slams his cock into me and my muscles instantly contract around him.

"God!" I call out as my orgasm takes over my whole body. My back arches, and my toes curl. Aiden moves in and out of my body fast and hard. His eyes stay fixated on our connection, watching as his cock pulls out of my body, coated in my juices. Within minutes, his movements become erratic and harder. He slams into me one last time and releases himself deep inside me.

His head rests on my chest while little tremors continue to work through his body.

"That was…" I whisper, not knowing the right words to finish that sentence. I'm not sure there are words to describe what he just did to me.

He shakes his head and gives me an adorable smirk. "I know," is all he says before pulling out of me and lifting me off the counter.

"Smug bastard," I mumble and pick up my clothes from the floor, putting them on.

"Oh, come on." His arms wrap around me, ceasing my movements. "You came so hard, you almost milked mine right out of me."

I harrumph and pretend to be offended even though I'm really not. It's hard to be pissed when you've just had a fantastic orgasm.

"Come on stud. Let's go to bed."

"Gladly," he whispers. His hand wraps around mine, and he leads me upstairs. Smug bastard or not… I still love him.

Jacob

Walking into our apartment, I hear pots and pans clanging and the melodious sounds of John Legend floating out from the kitchen. I round the corner and silently watch Kara as she gracefully moves around the room, humming and singing softly to the music.

This woman owns my heart and soul. There's nothing I wouldn't do for her. Just watching her performing mundane tasks like cooking, makes me feel calm and warm inside. She really is the best thing that has ever happened to me.

Her long, curly hair falls down her back. Her jeans are tight, highlighting each of her curves. And her sweater accentuates her perfect tits.

"You're home early," she murmurs while blowing on a spoonful of liquid. She brings the spoon to her mouth, and I watch as her little pink tongue snakes out to grab some sauce. Once she tastes it, she mumbles to herself, "Perfect."

"I am," I answer and close the distance between us, anxiously needing to feel her body against mine. My hand swipes her hair over her shoulder, and my mouth places soft, tender kisses down her neck. My arms tighten around her and draw her towards me so that her back is flush with my chest.

"Mmmm… I've missed you," she whispers. Her head tips to the side to give me better access to her neck.

"How much longer until dinner?" I ask as my mouth continues working along her neck. My tongue darts out to run along her earlobe, and I'm rewarded when a shudder moves through her body.

"Just another minute so hold those thoughts for later." She turns in my embrace and places a chaste kiss on my mouth. "Grab the plates and set the table."

Well shit. I guess that's that. Pouting, I open the cupboard and grab two plates. Next I open the drawer and grab silverware.

"You're cute when you pout. Did you know that?" Kara smiles as she teases me.

"How the hell do you do that?"

She raises her eyebrows and gives me a "What?" look.

"How did you know I was pouting when your back is to me?" It's like she has eyes in the back of her head. My mother was always like that, and it used to drive me crazy. God help our children if she's already honed her ability.

She shrugs and smiles. "I know you. That's all."

So true, Sunshine.

Sometimes I think she knows me better than I know myself.

Placing the dishes on the table, a song catches my attention on her iPod. I walk over and turn up the volume, wanting to hear the words better. When I realize how perfect this song is, I sweep Kara up into my arms, catching her off guard. I grab her hand and start swaying with her like the kitchen is our own personal dance floor. She giggles a little, but then places her head on my chest and melts into me. For the next three minutes, nothing else matters but Kara and me and the words of the song.

"This should be our wedding song," I announce, knowing she won't argue with me. Kara looks up with so much damn love in her eyes that a lump forms in my throat. Her smile says it all – she agrees with me that this is the perfect song.

"I couldn't agree more," she says softly. "The first time I heard it, I thought it was the most beautiful song ever. I couldn't be happier that you feel the same way."

Her chin quivers and her eyes fill with tears. Not to pat myself on the back or anything, but if you heard the words to this song, you would know that any woman would be bowled over by the sentiment. It's a sure fire way to get some action. It's not about the sex with Kara and me though. I can honestly say that each and every lyric in that song captures the essence of what I feel for her.

"All of me truly loves all of you, Kara." My fingers wipe away her tears and she gifts me with a wide smile. "I hope those are happy tears, Sunshine."

She laughs lightly and nods her head. Then taking a deep breath, she tells me, "Enough with the heavy shit. Let's eat."

A woman after my own heart.

Biting into the chicken, I can't help the moan I let out when the flavors burst on my tongue. If I'm not careful, Kara's cooking is going to make me gain weight. It's so damn rich and delicious, that I just can't help myself from indulging.

"I take it you like?" She asks teasingly, but I can tell the answer matters to her.

"You have no idea. The only thing better than this." I point at the plate with my knife. "Is tasting you."

Her cheeks flush and her eyelashes lower slightly. The hooded look of her eyes causes my stomach to stir with lust. Continuing to eat after that look is difficult, but I power through, looking forward to what's going to come after our meal.

"Oh my God! You'll never believe what happened to me today!" She exclaims a few minutes later. "I was shopping at the mall and I was in this shop filled with antique and handmade ornaments, when I dropped my phone without realizing it. So, I'm looking at these ornaments for Grace and Candace, and there's this tap on my shoulder. I turn around and – I shit you not – the guy holding my phone looked just like Santa Claus. I mean, *just like Santa.* It was so surreal that I almost died right there on the spot. All I wanted to do was sit on his lap and tell him what I wanted for Christmas. It's like I was compelled to do it. He looked at me like I was crazy. It was so wild."

"No shit?" I ask in disbelief. I wonder what it would be like to see good ole Kris Kringle. It must have been a blast back to her childhood for sure.

"Seriously. I felt like I was in a Hallmark movie or something." She looks at me hesitantly for a minute, biting her lip. It's as if she has something to say, but isn't sure how. "I was going to wait to tell you this, but in the spirit of Christmas I can't. I have some news," she finally says and then proceeds to keep eating, like she isn't leaving me hanging.

"Care to share?"

Her eyes blink, like she's trying to remember what she was talking about. I desperately want to laugh at her whenever she blanks out like that, but I fear it's a residual side effect of the attack and not just her being cute.

"Sorry. Right, well know how we were going to go to Colorado to spend Christmas with my parents?" I nod and she continues. "Well I talked to them today, and they are going to drive out here instead."

I sit back in my chair, both confused and elated with these turn of events. Meeting her parents for the first time will be a lot easier on my home turf. I'd be lying if I said I wasn't nervous about it. Honestly, I'm downright terrified. I know for a fact they weren't keen on my history with Brooke or the fact that I'm a police officer and have a "dangerous job."

"How come?" I ask curiously.

"Well, I couldn't see spending Christmas without Emma and the girls. Besides I think the girls would have been extremely sad to not have you there. For some odd and strange reason, they seem to worship the ground you walk on," she says cheekily.

Leave it to Kara to think about the girls' and my feelings and what me not being at Christmas would do to them. She really is something else. I know she was excited to go home and show me where she came from. Her doing this means the world to me. I really was a little upset about not getting to see the girls' faces on Christmas morning.

I lean over and kiss her long and hard. "Thank you," I say against her lips with as much sincerity as I can put in those two words.

"It was nothing really. My parents will be in town a week before Christmas so they'll stay here before we head to Pennsylvania. And Emma's already worked out the sleeping arrangements for her house."

"You're too good to be true." I reach down and pull her chair closer to mine. "I think I owe you some sexy time in order to show you my appreciation."

Her hands run up under my shirt, scorching my skin, as a look of pure lust crosses her face. "You do. I've been a very, very good girl and should be aptly rewarded."

Her teasing words are my undoing. I practically pounce on her, tackling her to the floor and pulling her shirt off. Her bra joins the shirt on the floor, allowing me to feast on her luscious breasts. My tongue circles the tips, making them pucker and beg for more attention. My fingers lightly stroke her under the waistband of her jeans, and her legs shift restlessly wanting more.

Ever the impatient one, my girl reaches down to undo her jeans and shimmy them down her legs. When her movements interrupt my ministrations, I release her breast and help pull her pants off. I toss them over my shoulder and spread her legs. I settle between them and nuzzle her inner thigh. The scent of her arousal fills my nostrils, making me crave a taste of her. My thumbs spread her wide, and my tongue runs teasingly along her skin and around her clit. I insert my tongue in her pussy and her legs clamp around my shoulders.

"Don't stop. Oh, please. Don't stop," she begs as my tongue flickers rapidly over her clit and I insert a finger into her hot and silky cunt.

I work my finger in and out of her slowly and match the rhythm with the flicks of my tongue. When her breathing is labored and her legs are trembling, I flatten my tongue against her clit and insert a second finger, stretching her wide. A simple crook of my fingers against her g-spot sends her into orbit. Her hands latch onto my hair, and her legs stiffen. My name tumbles from her lips over and over again, making me feel like king of the world.

I sit back on my knees and pull my shirt over my head. Next my fingers work swiftly on my jeans. Once I'm naked, I reach for Kara. She surprises me though by rolling on her stomach and sticking her ass enticingly in the air.

"I want you to take me from behind. I need you hard and deep tonight. I've been fantasizing about it for days. I hate when you put in a lot of hours at work and I don't get to see you."

My cock twitches and my balls tighten with her words, combined with the sight of her with her chest to the floor and her ass up in the air. She doesn't need to ask me twice.

Not wasting any time, I grab her hips and slam into her with one fast movement. My fingers dance up and down her spine as I take a moment to enjoy being buried balls deep in the sweetest pussy I've ever had. Ever the saucy minx, Kara rocks forward and slams back into me. I clench my muscles and grab her hips again before plunging in and out fast and hard – giving her exactly what she wanted.

"Fuck, baby. I'm not going to last long tonight," I grit out, knowing that I'm too primed to have a marathon session of sex.

"Mmm… ungh… oh…" Kara releases a bunch of non-sensical words. And that's when I realize her hand is working feverishly between her legs.

Damn that's fucking sexy.

I adjust the angle of my hips so that I'm driving into her deeper. The added friction I get from that change has my control disintegrating. I lose all concept of reality as my animal instincts take over, and I plow into her savagely.

Kara starts convulsing underneath me, and her pussy sucks me in over and over with her release. My balls tighten in answer, and my spine stiffens straight as a rod. A shout leaves my lips as I come deep inside her. Idly, my hand strokes over her ass cheeks as my brain attempts to un-scramble itself.

Mind-blowing. Each and every damn time with her is like an out of body experience. I don't know what I did to be this damn lucky.

Chapter Three

Sam

"Come on, baby," I murmur as I straighten the strap of the diaper bag on my shoulder and grip Tessa's hand tighter. Now that she's walking it is so hard to get her to let me carry her. Most times I don't mind it, but today I'm running late to meet Aiden for lunch. I detest being late, even if it is just for lunch with my husband. It sends the message that your time is more important than theirs when you're late. However, I had promised the girls in his office holiday cookies, and then got stuck waiting for the last batch to cool before I could package them. Aiden might have eaten a few too many between Saturday and today. I threatened to cut him off from sex if he didn't stop messing with my cookies. That quickly curbed his behavior.

"Wawawoopsie mommy!" Tessa shrieks and starts struggling against my hold. I turn to see that five feet back, her doll lies on the floor. Crocodile tears start pouring down her cheeks.

Shit.

"Go get her, baby." I release her hand and watch as her little legs run towards her doll. She picks Jewel up and cradles her in her arms and kisses her head. God, she's so damn cute.

"Come on. We have to go get daddy."

Tessa's eyes widen, and a smile graces her face. Her tears are long since forgotten at the mention of Aiden. She runs back to me, grabbing my hand.

"Good girl," I murmur with a smile on my face. I push open the glass door to the office of McGee, Smith, Rodman & Associates and am greeted by the receptionist Penny.

"Mrs. Parker! How are you? Oh and you brought darling Tessa with you!" My smile widens as she scurries out from behind the desk.

"Hi Penny. Could you take these for me?" I point to the bag with the packages of cookies in it that hangs from my arm with the diaper bag.

Tessa takes my distraction as the perfect opportunity to run towards the hall where Aiden's office is. Penny grabs the bag as I turn to chase after my speed demon daughter. When I round the corner into Aiden's office, I stop dead in my tracks. Aiden scooches his chair further back from the desk and picks up a babbling Tessa. But that isn't what has me frozen to my spot in the doorway. No... the culprit for that is a shapely, attractive woman wearing a tight, white blouse with cleavage spilling out and a tight, red skirt. She's sitting on the edge of Aiden's desk – close to him – with her long, attractive legs crossed in his direction.

What the hell did I just walk in on?

The woman in question tosses her long, black hair over her shoulder and grins a catty grin at me, before turning to ooh and ah over Tessa.

"Aiden," my voice betrays my displeaswithe in the situation. Damn it. I don't want to be one of those women. Especially given my history.

"Hi, honey. Have you met Rocky? She's the new architect McGee hired," he gestures over to the woman who has that catty grin on her face again.

This is Rocky? Unless she has it tucked up real good, there is no way Rocky sports a dick. I feel foolish for assuming he's been taking late night calls from and spending days off with a man, when all along it's been this... this woman.

My blood boils knowing I'm going to have to be polite to her. It goes against every one of my instincts to be nice right now.

"Hello. I'm Samantha," I graciously introduce myself to her and pretend that she isn't attempting to flash my husband her boobs and legs right in front of me.

"Pleasure to meet you, Samantha. I've heard a lot about you." She stands and walks over to where Aiden has now joined me. She rests her hand on his arm and leans subtly towards him. "I'll just be going. We can finish our discussion later."

Her words ooze innuendo, and I have visions of dragging her out of the room by her hair and throwing her down a flight of stairs.

"Sure, no problem," Aiden responds, not paying attention to her now that Tessa is wriggling to get down.

I watch in shock as she struts – yes, struts – out of his office on four inch heels and down the hall. My body is reverberating with pure, unadulterated rage. My first instinct is to lash out at Aiden for being so damn inappropriate and putting himself in a precarious position, but that would be hypocritical of me... wouldn't it?

"What's wrong?" Aiden asks. His head is cocked to the side, and he is studying me intently.

"Nothing," I lie and turn to gather Tessa. "You ready to go?"

"We can leave once you stop trying to bullshit me. Your face is pale and you look like you're ready to spit nails."

Well, I guess I'm going to be forced to do this...

"I cannot believe I walked in here to find you cozied up with that woman on your desk!" I realize my voice is rising, so I walk over and close his door. No one needs to witness this show.

"First of all, I don't know what you are talking about. She just wanted to bounce some design ideas she had off of me. Rocky's friendly, that's all." He shrugs and I want to throw something at his head for being so obtuse. "Second of all, hello pot... meet kettle! I can't believe you are acting like this."

"Oh, that's rich! Throw my mistakes in my face, why don't you? She practically rubbed against you like a cat in heat!" I sputter indignantly.

"She did not! That's just crazy talk. Listen... I didn't mean to throw the past in your face, but even you have to admit you are being a bit hypocritical right now. You need to trust me."

I drop my head in defeat and pinch the bridge of my nose. I can feel the tears start to prick the back of my eyes. If Aiden were to stray, it would be nothing less than what I deserve. There is no way I can compete with 'Miss No Cellulite.' She is dressed like a Porsche while I'm standing here dressed like a Honda, in jeans and an oversized sweater. No man wants an old, reliable car when he can drive a flashy, fast machine. Shit... I probably have animal crackers stuck in my hair still! That's not attractive!

Gah! I can't believe this is happening! I can't compete with that!

"I'm sorry. I didn't mean to upset you. You have absolutely nothing to worry about. Rocky is just overly friendly. I promise you there is nothing going on with her. She knows I'm married. You're just being paranoid." Aiden tries to appease me, but he falls flat with that last statement.

"Paranoid?" I ask quietly. He'd be an idiot not to pick up on my displeasure right now.

"Okay... maybe that was a poor choice of words. I just meant you should trust me. You're reading into this more than you should."

Tears fill my eyes, and I want to run and hide so he doesn't see them. Damn hormones!

"Awww... Don't cry," he croons in my ear as he wraps me up in his strong, lean arms. His touch calms me and I quickly stifle my tears.

"You okay?" He leans back and assesses my face. I nod my head in answer to his question.

"Good. Let's grab 'wild thing' over here and go get some lunch." He points over to his desk. I laugh at the sight of Tessa with the wastebasket tipped over and papers everywhere. She sure knows the most quick and efficient ways to make a mess.

After we pick up the mess and grab our things, I square my shoulders and follow Aiden out of his office. We stop at his boss, McGee's, office and I kiss the man's cheek when he stands to greet us. Tessa rests on my hip and leans in to copy my movements. The old grinch's eyes light up and his wrinkled, hard face actually breaks out into a grin. I swear I haven't seen him grin in years. It's a Christmas miracle!

"She's quite the darling," he grumbles and walks back to his desk. "You take care now."

Well... I guess we've been dismissed.

"Merry Christmas!" I call out as I leave his office.

Next stop is at Diane's desk. Diane is the secretary for all the partners. She is sixty, yet looks like she's forty. I could only hope to look half as good as she does when I'm her age. I'm convinced that she and Rodman have something going on. Aiden says he has never seen them be inappropriate, but the heated looks they give each other when they think no one is watching is quite obvious.

"Thank you so much for the cookies!" Diane exclaims exuberantly. "You're a doll!"

After visiting for a few minutes, Aiden takes Tessa down the hall to play with the toys that Penny keeps in her desk.

"So what's bothering you," Diane asks with concern in her eyes.

"How did you know?"

"You look tired and stressed out, dear. You can tell me if you want. It won't go past these walls." She rests her hands on mine and encourages me to open up to her. Diane is the mother I wish I had. I tell her everything… within reason of course.

"What do you know about this Rocky chick?" I ask and feel my face flame with embarrassment. I don't want people to think I can't keep my husband satisfied.

"Oh, her," Diane's voice falls flat and the concern on her face intensifies. "I wouldn't trust her if I were you. She's been sniffing around the men in this office something fierce. If I were twenty or thirty years younger, I'd take her down a peg or two."

My stomach twists at her warning. This is what I was afraid of. Aiden might be oblivious to her intentions, but she made them quite clear to me with her behavior earlier in his office.

"She calls him late at night and he went out to meet her at a site last weekend on his day off. I didn't realize she was a woman until I met her today. I walked in on her sitting on his desk. She was practically in his lap and then she had the nerve to touch him in front of me." I seethe at the memory.

Diane's hand squeezes mine gently. "Aiden has never shown her any attention outside of being professional and friendly."

I know her words are meant to reassure, but I'm all too familiar with what can happen when temptation is dangled in front of you. My imagination races with images of her stripping for him in his office and him caving at the sight of a beautiful, naked woman in front of him. Tears well up in my eyes. I can't curse my hormones enough today.

"Honey, don't cry. Will it make you feel better if I keep an eye on things for you?" She hands me a tissue, and I wipe my tears before blowing my nose.

"Would you?" I ask sheepishly. I know I shouldn't be dragging Diane into my insecurities, but it will make me feel better.

"Sure thing, hon. Now go find that sexy husband of yours and get out of here. Penny already passed out the cookies to everyone, so there's no need to linger. Go and enjoy yourself!"

I stand and hug her, thankful for having a woman like her in my life. My own mother never would have been able to make me feel better. She would have told me to hire a private detective to catch him having an affair and then divorce his ass and take him for all he's worth. *Such wisdom she possesses...*

Aiden and Tessa are in his friend Ben's office when I finally locate them.

"Hey, Ben!" I greet him with a hug. You'd think Aiden and Ben were related with how similar they look, but they've been friends since elementary school.

"You look as beautiful as ever, Sam," he kisses my cheek and winks at me.

"You're such a smooth talker. I'm going to have to warn Charlotte!" I say referring to Ben's wife. When I perch myself on Aiden's lap, he grips my hips and makes me yelp.

"Will you stop?" My stomach grumbles and I place my hand over my belly.

"We should probably get going so we can feed that beast in your belly," Aiden announces with a laugh and pushes me off his lap before standing.

"Let me just kiss my goddaughter," Ben says, bending down to pick up Tessa. She nuzzles into his neck and gives him a big hug.

"See you later," we call out as we leave the office. Thankfully, I didn't have to see that floozy bitch again.

Chapter Four

Kara

"Miss Andrews?"

I look up from my computer screen to see Jerome standing in my doorway with his hands in his pockets, biting his lip nervously.

"What's up, Jerome?" I ask with what I hope is a warm smile on my face.

"I… I got you something for Christmas." He looks down at the ground and rocks back on his heels. "Since you're going on vacation, I wanted to give it to you now. If that's okay, I mean."

"Oh, Jerome! Of course it's okay!"

His eyes look up from the carpet, and he gives me a tentative smile.

"It isn't much, but I saw it and thought of you." He walks over to my desk and hands me a small, green and red wrapped box.

I quickly tear into the paper, excited that he gave me a gift. Each year, I give the kids little gifts, but I don't usually get too many in return. Not that I expect them or anything. But when I do get them, it makes it that much more special.

Once the paper is gone, I open up the plain, white box. Pulling out the delicate ornament, I'm speechless. It's a light green, round ball shaped ornament. Hand painted shamrocks wrap around the entirety of it, along with a gorgeous, redheaded Irish dancer. How very thoughtful of him. I love all things Irish, but he couldn't have known that.

"Wow, Jerome. It's lovely. Thank you so much! I love Irish ornaments." I jump up from the chair and round my desk to stand in front of him. "You are quite a considerate young man. Thank you again."

I give him a quick hug and am surprised when he hugs me back tightly.

"Miss Andrews…" He trails off, and I have a feeling I know where this is going. Poor thing still feels guilty over what happened last year.

"Don't. I'm serious, Jerome. We've gone over this a hundred times. You couldn't have known and I'm fine now." I lean back to look him in the face and give him a tight squeeze before releasing him.

"Okay," he concedes with a small grin.

"I'm giving the rest of the kids their presents tonight, but here." I hand him a card from the stack on my desk. "You can have yours now."

He gives me a wide smile and opens the card. "Wicked! A gift card to Best Buy!"

There are a handful of kids that I give a little more to. They are the ones that I work with on a regular basis. Given mine and Jerome's history I gave him more than I probably should have. But he really was trying to save me that day. He was just trying to save me from the wrong man. The fact that he cared enough, gives him a special place in my heart.

"Thanks Miss Andrews! I better get home. My grandma is coming to visit for Christmas and mom says I need to help get the house ready."

"You're welcome and have a Merry Christmas. Tell your mom the same."

"I will," he says on his way out the door.

I don't know what I would do without my kids. They mean the world to me. I sigh and sit back down to finish my work. I need to get home so Jacob and I can decorate the tree!

When I got home from work, Jacob wasn't home yet. I was too excited to wait to decorate the apartment, so I cranked up the Christmas playlist on my iPod and went to town. Our living room and kitchen are now a virtual Christmas wonderland.

There are Christmas themed cookie jars, salt and pepper shakers, towels, and decorative bowls scattered throughout the kitchen. The table runner has been replaced and a big bowl of Christmas tree scented potpourri sits on top of it. A Christmas table runner garnishes the dining room table and for a centerpiece, I filled a glass vase with ornaments. Simple, easy and elegant.

The living room is decked out with lighted garland and decorative pillows. Jacob's leather chair has a Christmas quilt draped over it. Then I took an oversized bowl and filled it with more potpourri and giant Christmas bulbs to adorn the coffee table. I hung strands of white lights around the picture window and the sliding glass doors. The fireplace mantel has a Christmas wreath over it and lighted garland along the top. I put some nice candlesticks up there as well. They flank an old, ceramic snowman that my grandmother gave to my mother when she was a young girl. And of course, I hung our stockings from the mantel. I absolutely love having a fireplace to hang stockings from.

The door closes, and I spin around enthusiastically. Jacob whistles as he walks into the room.

"Was I that late? You have just about everything done."

"Sorry. I got a little carried away." I bounce on my feet like I'm five waiting for Santa to come down the chimney.

"How much sugar have you had today?" Jacob laughs and wraps me in his arms for a kiss.

"Um… I might have had like six candy canes," I admit begrudgingly.

"I think it's cute how excited you are. It's our first proper Christmas together. I want you to go crazy decorating the place."

"Good. Now get your coat off and help me with the tree!" I exclaim and pick up a strand of white lights to hold out to him.

He chuckles and shakes his head like I have a screw loose, but takes his coat off and joins me.

"So how was your day?" I ask as we take turns passing the strand of lights around the width of the tree.

The tree we picked out last night is thick and lush. It's the most ideal Christmas tree you could hope to find. Not too wide, not too tall, not too sparse but not too full. It's just right.

"Same shit, different day. I asked Mack today if he wanted to come to Emma's for Christmas with us, but he said he had other plans."

"I thought you said he didn't have any family around here."

"He doesn't. I'm sure he has friends though. Maybe he's spending it with them."

"Well, as long as he isn't alone on Christmas. It would break my heart if he didn't have anyone to spend the day with. He's been so great to me, and I couldn't bear the thought of him alone." Mack is like a brother to me after everything I went through. He was there for Jacob, and he constantly checked in on me. I can't count the number of times he chauffeured me around before the attack keeping me safe, and how many times he brought me magazines and snacks when I was recovering.

Jacob walks over and kisses me thoroughly. "And that is one of the many things I love about you. Your big, giving heart," he says once he pulls away from me.

"That's sweet, babe. Thank you." I blush at his compliment.

"So your parents will be here tomorrow night. You excited?" He takes the lights from my hand and pulls them around to his side of the tree.

"For as much as I miss them, I'm not sure excited is the right word to use. Do you have any idea how hard it was to convince them to not bring Fiona with them?"

"Fiona?" Jacob murmurs as he climbs under the tree to plug in the lights.

"The latest addition to their marriage. Remember I told you about her? Apparently my dad brought her into the marriage and my mother decided to share as well. So, yeah. Basically they are branching out into threesomes now. I swear I'll never understand those two."

"Why didn't you want her to come? What if *she's* going to be all alone at Christmas?" He looks up at me from under the tree.

"Don't give me that shit, Jacob. I already made sure she had somewhere else to go before I put my foot down. Could you imagine all three of them meeting your family on Christmas? No. Not going to happen. There's no way I could stand trying to explain that one to Grace and Candace."

"Look, Sunshine. Just because she'd be with them doesn't mean they would have had to sleep in the same room. Maybe your issues with the whole open marriage thing are clouding your judgment on this one." He stands up and puts his hands on my shoulders.

I huff and refrain from decking him. Of course he's right. But that doesn't mean I'm changing my mind. For years growing up, I felt like my parents' play friends were more important than me. The fact that they agreed not to bring Fiona, means the world to me. Whatever floats their boat is fine. I just don't want it shoved down my throat any longer. A lifetime of it has been enough.

"Can we change the subject please?" I plead with him. I don't want to fight while wrapped up in Christmas cheer.

"Sure. How did your last day before vacation go?" Jacob thankfully changes the subject.

"Great actually. Oh! Wait until you see the ornament Jerome got me!" I race over to my bag and dig out the box.

"Jerome?" Jacob asks as he reaches down and starts grabbing ornaments out of the plastic containers I store them in.

"Yeah, look." I hold it out and he spins the bulb looking at it.

"Wow. The girl looks just like you."

"You think?" I ask, spinning it back around to look at the dancer. "Huh. I guess she does. That's so cool!"

Jacob laughs and shakes his head. "You're a nut."

"Takes one to know one," I zing back lamely.

Once all the ornaments are all hung on the tree, I hand the Belleek Irish porcelain star to Jacob to set on top of the tree. *I told you I liked Irish stuff.* He reaches up and gently sets it on top. When he stands back to admire the tree, he wraps his arm around my shoulder and I lean my head on his chest.

Turning in his embrace, I wrap my arms around his neck and pull him down for a sensual kiss. I step back and reach for the hem of my sweater, pulling it over my head.

Jacob's eyes glaze over and the corners of his mouth tip up slightly.

"Want to have some fun under the Christmas tree?" I ask while tracing my finger over the edges of my pink, lace bra.

His growl is the only answer I get before he tackles me to the ground and proceeds to make love to me slowly and sweetly while the lights twinkle around us.

"Thanks for going shopping with me today," Sophie says as she rubs a hand over her swollen belly.

"It was nothing. I'm not sure you could have managed on your own," I joke even though I had my concerns numerous times throughout the day.

"I know," she chuckles softly. "This baby is sucking the life out of me. I can't wait for my due date next week."

Truth be told, I can't wait for her due date either. I'm longing to get my hands on her and Brad's baby. There is no way in hell he won't be the cutest little thing ever given their genetics. I haven't told Jacob, but I think my biological clock is starting to tick. It physically hurts to see little babies and their moms. Sometimes I just want to weep with the need inside me. Crazy, right?

"Wouldn't it be wild if you have a Christmas baby? I always thought it would be cool to be born on a holiday."

"In theory. Could you imagine how much it would suck to only get presents once though? I'm sure plenty of kids get screwed and only get a regular amount of gifts, when in reality they'd get more if their birthday was in say, June."

I nod my head in agreement. That is a very good point. I'm glad my birthday is in August. That would have sucked big time.

"So what are you getting Jacob? You didn't really buy too much today." Sophie picks up her tea and sips it, before leaning back and continuing to rub her belly.

"Well, I spent way more than I should have. I wanted to get him a new gun, but I have no idea what is good in a gun. It's not like I could pick one that is pretty, because really guns are supposed to be manly and they all look similar. And I have not one clue what makes a gun work good, so I asked Mack to help me. He took me to a gun emporium and rambled off a bunch of stuff that I paid absolutely no attention to before he handed me one and said, 'This should do it'. It's a pretty kick ass looking gun."

The claim that I spent too much is an understatement really. The fact that Jacob refuses to let me pay half the bills helped me save quite a bit of money, but I ended up dipping into my savings seeing as how he had to have accessories like a night sight and a holster. I might have gone a touch overboard. I'm not too worried about it though, because he's worth every last penny.

Sophie throws her head back and laughs. "Thank God you had Mack. I can just imagine you trying to tell a salesperson what you were looking for. 'Hello, one kick ass gun please.' Man, Kara, you're too funny."

I shrug and sip my coffee. "It is pretty kick ass. Just saying."

"I'm sure he'll love it. Have you snooped for your presents yet?" Her eyes dance with mischief.

"No. I don't like my surprises to be ruined, 'Miss I Know Exactly What I'm Getting For Christmas'."

"Brad needs all the help he can get sometimes. He doesn't do well in that department. After the first couple of years together, I learned to just make him a list with exact instructions of what to get me. It saves me from having to return the stuff later on."

I laugh and shake my head. "You are so bad!"

"I know!" She joins in and ends up laughing so hard, she has to run to the bathroom to keep from peeing her pants.

"Alright. Time to go spend some more money!" She exclaims when she arrives back at the table.

"Let's do this thing!" I reply as I follow her out into the cold with a little pep in my step. I so can't wait for Christmas.

Chapter Five

Sam

"I need to get my hands on one of those damn Big Hugs Elmos," I mumble, aggravated as I scour the ads in the paper. I feel like Christmas shopping has become a game in this day and age. It sure ain't like it was when we were younger, that's for sure. Now there's online shopping, stores opening on Thanksgiving, everyone hunting for that elusive deal, and so on. It's enough to drive a girl batty.

"Don't you think the gifts already in the closet are more than enough?" Aiden asks with his gaze fixed on the football game.

"Easy for you to say. You never put any input into the gifts. I'm the one who gets stuck fixating on every damn detail. What should we get for so-and-so? How much should we spend on each person? Am I getting the best deal? Maybe I should get this instead of that. You just sit there and watch fucking football!" I rant and finish by slamming my hand along with the flyer on the coffee table.

Aiden turns his head towards me and raises his eyebrows until they are practically in his hairline. "Seems a bit much for some Christmas presents, don't you think?"

"Oh... you... Gah!" I stand up and make to leave the room. Aiden's fingers wrap around my wrists, halting my progress. He stands and leads me with his hands on my shoulders to the closet in the family room. He opens the door, and I cringe at what I know is coming.

"Sam, look at all these presents that you already bought for her," he speaks slowly, like I'm a caged animal he's afraid to spook. "Tessa doesn't need all these things. Hell, we barely have room for all her toys now. Tell me what's really going on."

"I just wanted it to be special for her. Don't you get it?" I implore with him to see things my way for once. I hate that he is the rational one between us. And there is no way I'm telling him exactly why I think Tessa needs to be spoiled.

"She's two. She isn't going to remember all this. You have at least a dozen puzzles here, coloring books, crayons, a toy kitchen set, four new LaLaLoopsie dolls, an American Girl doll, and a damn Leap Pad. And that isn't counting all these clothes. Again, she's two. What is she going to do with a Leap Pad?" He stops rifling through all the packages and turns to look at me, waiting for his answer.

"She'll be able to read books on the Leap Pad, asshole," I grumble in self-defense. "Besides, I still remember the day my father made me throw out my first baby blanket. I was her age and I still remember. So there!" I stick my hand on my cocked hip, showing my stubbornness.

"That was a traumatizing event, which is probably why you remember it. Christmas is a happy time," he continues to argue.

"Well yeah, if you get all the right toys. Otherwise, we could be doing real damage to our daughter, Aiden. Do you want her to look back and say, 'I still remember the year my parents didn't love me enough to get me any presents on Christmas'?"

Aiden rolls his eyes and looks to the ceiling, like he is praying for strength. Or maybe he is praying for a divine intervention. Regardless... he isn't going to win this one.

"You already got her more than enough presents. I don't want to picture you in a store, elbowing and cursing while you fight tooth and nail for a damn Elmo doll that will hug our daughter. *That* isn't what Christmas is about."

I just stare at him, not responding to his last comment. I know he's right, but that doesn't change the fact that I'm going to get our daughter one of those damn Elmos come hell or high water. Once I get something in my head, rarely does it leave without me acting on it.

"If you get arrested, just know I won't bail you out. You can figure that one out on your own." He shakes his head and walks away, knowing I'm not going to change my mind.

I smile victoriously and make my way to the phone book. I pick up the phone and begin dialing the local stores that sell the Elmo doll, asking when they are expecting their next shipment. Over the next few days, Tessa and I will be on the hunt for one.

Jacob

I wipe my sweaty palms on my khaki pants and continue pacing the length of the living room. Kara's parents are going to be here any minute. Normally, I would have picked them up at the airport, but her mom is deathly afraid of flying so they are driving in from Colorado.

I must say, I'm surprised at how nervous I am to be meeting them. I've spoken to Bill and Margaret Andrews numerous times on the phone. Last year when Kara was brutally beaten, I spoke to them every day in order to update them on her progress. I know my reaction to this introduction is ridiculous, but I can't seem to help it.

Kara walks out of the bedroom in a body hugging, green sweater dress and I pause my movement to watch her. My God, she's the most beautiful thing I've ever seen.

She tosses her hair over her shoulder and tips her head to the side as her fingers hook in her earring. My gaze travels down over the curves that I know oh so well and ends at her killer stilettos. I'd work hundreds of hours of overtime to buy her more shoes that look like that.

"If you keep looking at me like that, my parents are going to catch us in a compromising position," Kara mutters to me while latching on her other earring.

"You even make the word position sound dirty, Sunshine. All I can think about is bending you over the couch now."

"Well at least I've taken your mind off meeting my parents. You've practically worn a hole in the rug pacing back and forth on it."

Hmmm... she might be right about that. I'm thankful for the reprieve from my jitters, but I don't want to have a semi meeting her parents for the first time either.

Kara walks over to me and wraps her arms around my neck. My hands settle on her waist and draw her closer to me. Her floral scent has me wanting to bury my nose in her neck to sniff her.

"It will be okay. My parents already like you. This is just a formality," she reassures me in between soft, light kisses.

"They weren't thrilled when they found out I was engaged to Brooke before you," I remind her and nip her lips with my teeth. "Or the fact that, what did your mom say? Oh, right... 'that I could end up filled with bullet holes in my line of work.'"

"That was before you took such good care of me after the whole Cory incident. Now I'm pretty sure they think you're a saint." Her hands lower and run over my chest, where they start playing with the end of my tie... so damn close to the promise land.

"You do realize you're giving me a hard-on when your parents are going to be here any minute."

She jumps back and puts distance between us. "Shit. Sorry."

I shake my head and scrub my hands down my face. "It's fine. I'll just think of dead puppies or something."

"Speaking of puppies. I talked to Emma today and I guess the girls fell in love with the puppies that the next door neighbor is selling. I told her we'd buy them one for Christmas." She walks over to her cell phone and scrolls through it before handing it to me. My heart tugs when I look at the picture of two golden retriever puppies lying together. One has his paw thrown over the neck of the other as they snuggle together.

"Get both," I announce and hand her back the phone.

"Both?" She asks with a hint of surprise in her voice.

"I want each of the girls to have one. And I want it to be those two. They remind me of Emma and me. And Grace and Candace."

"I'm not sure Emma wanted to take on two dogs, Jacob." Kara tries to reason with me.

"I don't care. She should have thought about that before proposing the idea. Get both of them."

"Oooookay," she drags the word out in disbelief. She should know by now that when I make up my mind about something, I don't generally change it afterward.

A knock on the door ends the conversation, and Kara's rushes to open it. I join her as the door opens and her parents enthusiastically hug their daughter.

"Jacob," her father greets me and shakes my hand as he moves past Kara. He's a good looking older man with salt and pepper hair. He looks scholarly in his tweed coat and Fedora. I suppose that's to be expected considering he is a professor at a university.

"Mr. Andrews," I return his greeting and step back to let him into the apartment.

"Please, call me Bill." He walks into the room and surveys the apartment.

"Mrs. Andrews," I greet Kara's mother with a kiss on her cheek. They say if you want to know what a woman will look like when she is older, then look at her mother. Well, I'm pleased to announce that if that's true, then Kara will be one fine looking woman when she's her mother's age. Her mother is the spitting image of her, but thirty years older. Hardly any wrinkles are present on her face, and she is svelte and fashionable.

"Maggie, please. No Mrs. Andrews from you." She stands back and appraises me with eagle eyes. "My, my Kara. You certainly did well for yourself. Your fiancé is quite the looker."

"He is, isn't he," Kara sighs and wraps her arms around my waist, resting her head on my chest.

"Let me take your bags." I grab their suitcases and bring them down the hall, leaving Kara to have a few moments with her parents before we go to dinner.

After setting their suitcases in the guest room, I grab my wallet and keys from our bedroom and head out to the living room.

Rounding the doorway into the hall, I abruptly stop when Kara's father blocks the way. He stands there with his arms crossed and silently stares at me. My throat works as I attempt to swallow. I feel like I'm meeting the boogeyman in a dark alleyway.

"Sir?" I ask when he doesn't speak right away. I can feel his eyes as they assess me, and I hope I don't come up lacking. I couldn't bear for her parents not to like me. I know she's too good for me, but I plan on spending the rest of my life busting my ass to be worthy of her.

"I just wanted to thank you, son. Kara is our world, whether she believes that or not. If you hadn't been there for her when that animal attacked her..." His eyes glaze over and his words drift off like he's imagining the worst. He clears his throat and continues, "Let's just say, I don't know how we would have handled that. I believe she's in good hands with you and I couldn't be happier that the two of you are getting married. Welcome to the family."

He shakes my hand again, and I feel a weight lift off my shoulders. It feels good to have her parents' approval.

"Thank you, sir. I promise I'll always take care of her."

"I believe that. Now let's go to dinner. I could eat a horse, I'm so damn hungry."

"Then we should definitely get going." I let out a little chuckle and hold my arm out, signaling for him to precede me down the hall.

Lying on my back, Kara's head rests on my chest. Her fingers draw random patterns on my chest. The moonlight streams in through the window, highlighting the beauty of her. My hand tightens on her hip, thinking about having her naked body fully displayed in the moonlight.

"My parents are definitely in love with you," she speaks softly into the silence.

"I'm glad. They seem like good people. I'm looking forward to getting to know them better over the next week or so." I'm still a little fuzzy on how long her parents are staying with us after Christmas. Kara asked them at dinner tonight, but her mother changed the subject.

"Dinner went well. I think my dad really liked the restaurant. Taking him somewhere that he could get a giant steak was a good idea."

"Sunshine, he's a man. Of course I knew steak would go over well." I chuckle at her observation.

"Well, whatever." She huffs before going back to drawing on my chest with her fingertips.

Dinner did go rather well. After her father surprised the shit out of me by giving me his blessing, it was easy to be relaxed with him and Maggie. I even learned a little more about Fiona and their unconventional relationship, thanks to her parents' loose lips. I can see why Kara squirms and gets upset whenever she's confronted with the oddity of their marriage. They are just so open and forthcoming with details that most people would find extremely personal. At one point, I cringed when I thought her mother was going to explain the physicality of some of their encounters with Fiona… if you catch my drift.

"I can't believe you're getting the girls each a puppy." Kara thankfully breaks me from thoughts about kinky threesomes and her parents.

"They should each have their own. That way they won't fight over the thing and they'll both have to learn some responsibility."

Kara laughs and reminds me that my sister is going to kill me. "Emma is not going to be happy with you. I sent her a text asking for the phone number of the breeders so that I could talk to them myself. I figured we were better off surprising her as well."

"Good call. Once the girls have them, she won't be able to say no. She might threaten to cut my balls off, but at least the girls will already have the dogs." I semi-joke.

"Hey, I like your balls thank you very much. Let's see what we can do about keeping them intact."

"That sounds like a perfect plan." Staring at the ceiling, I feel my eyelids getting heavy as we do our now routine pillow talk.

"I'm taking my parents on a tour of D.C. tomorrow. My dad wants to see the White House all decked for Christmas. This is the first time they've ever been here."

"That will be fun. I have to go into the station tomorrow, but I'll make sure I'm home for dinner." I kiss the top of her head and close my eyes.

"I'm going to make pot roast for dinner. I figure I'll stick it in the crockpot before we leave so that it has time to cook. I know how much you like my pot roast."

"Hmmm… I do," I mumble, feeling myself start to fall asleep. I love just about anything Kara makes.

"Goodnight, babe." Kara scoots up and kisses my cheek. I turn my head and capture her lips with mine for a brief, but thorough, exploration of her mouth.

"Goodnight, Sunshine." I tuck her into my side and sigh contentedly. It's moments like these that I cherish the most.

Chapter Six

Jacob

Visiting in-laws, or soon to be in-laws in my case, are the biggest cockblock I've witnessed in my nearly thirty-six years of life. Let's look back at how this last week has gone for me, shall we?

First block – in the middle of a heated make out session, hoping you can get your girl to go a little further because she's so into the moment, and her mom knocks on the bedroom door to ask us if we want breakfast.

Second block – getting arguably the best head of your life and you let out a groan that is beyond your control at the time, causing your girl stop because her dad is a light sleeper and you're being too loud.

Third block – your girl just came with your head between her legs, and you're in the middle of crawling up her body so you can plunge into her wet heat, when her parents choose that exact moment to have a conversation in the hall right outside your door.

All these things add up to the biggest case of blue balls I've ever experienced. I feel so bad for my poor dick that I'm ready to throw him a pity party. He's sick of my hand abusing him in the shower.

But tonight… Tonight, I'm putting an end to this. I'm making love to my girl, and I don't care if her parents walk in the room mid-thrust. We are seeing this through start to finish this time.

Okay. I will concede that maybe that was a little crude, but there is only so much a man can take.

I look around the room and survey my handywork. Candles lit? Check. Television turned on low enough to mute sounds but not be distracting? Check. Handcuffs secured to the bed? Check. Scarf ready? Check. Painful erection thanks to imagining Kara sprawled out naked on the bed? Check.

The bathroom door opens and steam wafts out around Kara's stunningly half naked body. She's reminiscent of an angel descending from heaven. My eyes rake over her body, starting with the hair that is pulled up in a knot on the top of her head, following down to where her nipples are poking out of her tight, white tank top, then finding her skimpy white, laced underwear, lingering around her long, slender legs and finishing with her pink painted toes. If I wasn't hard before, I would be now. My girl is quite a fox. And the best part is, she doesn't even realize it.

"What are you looking at?" Kara asks with a blush covering her cheeks at my scrutiny.

"You are so damn beautiful, Sunshine. You take my breath away."

I cross the distance between us and wrap her in my arms and carry her to the bed. I lay her down gently and step back to look my fill. Keeping eye contact, I push my sweatpants down my legs and kick them off. Her eyes widen, and her tongue snakes out to wet her lips. *Yeah my girl likes what she sees too.*

Next I slowly lower my boxers down my legs. I palm my erection, all the while keeping eye contact with Kara.

"Jacob, I don't know if we should," she says in reaction to my forward actions. Then lower she says, "My parents are in the next room."

I kneel on the bed and lean over her to give her a long, deep, wet kiss. Once I know her brain is thoroughly scrambled and thinking about that kiss rather than her parents, I pull her arms up over the pillows and latch the handcuffs around her each of her wrists. I sit back when she starts pulling on the cuffs.

"What the...?" She asks eyeing the metal around her wrists. "This isn't funny. You need to undo these right now."

I figure in for a penny, in for a pound. I grab the scarf from the night stand and wrap it around her head, covering her mouth with it. I tie it behind her head and run my fingertips over her jaw and down her neck.

Her ensuing words are muffled due to the silky material currently acting as a gag on her. Her eyes widen and fear flashes in her baby blues.

"Shhh... I won't hurt you. You know that, Sunshine. This is for you. I want you to enjoy what I'm about to do without worrying about being loud or trying to stop it because of your parents. Let me take care of you, sweetheart." My hands run soothingly over her bare skin in an attempt to take her mind off of being bound by me.

Once I feel her body relax, I move my mouth lightly over her jaw and down her neck. My mouth and tongue work over her collarbone and down to her cleavage. My fingers drag the material of her tank top slowly up her torso and over her breasts, exposing her to me. I can feel her heart start to beat faster, and her breathing becomes shallow and erratic.

Taking a nipple in my mouth, I start off sucking softly, slowly increasing my pressure. All the while, my hand fondles her other breast. My thumb and forefinger pinch and roll her nipple. Switching breasts, I continue to torment her. Loving her soft, breathy moans and the way her legs open wider, silently asking me for more.

I take my time, exploring every part of her body that I can get to. The way she writhes under me, undulating her hips against my erection, has me wanting to speed this up. I am taking a huge chance of being interrupted by going slow, but I feel like it's necessary. I need to do it this way. It wouldn't feel right after everything that's happened to Kara for me to tie her up and treat her roughly. I cherish the fact that she trusts me enough to let me take her freedom and control away. I'd never abuse that trust.

Slipping my fingers in the sides of her panties, I draw them down her leg and toss them over my shoulder. I nuzzle the soft curls between her legs and inhale the scent of her arousal. My dick throbs wanting to be buried deep inside her. But instead of listening to it, I swipe my tongue through her folds and taste Kara's sweetness. As my tongue circles her clit, I work first one, then two fingers inside her. Looking up at her face and seeing the rapture she's caught up in, has me almost coming as I press my cock into the bed, needing the friction to take the edge off my need.

When her muscles spasm and her orgasm rolls through her, I gently continue working between her legs, bringing her down. Truth be told, I can't get enough of the sweet taste. I could spend days between her legs if given the chance.

I move up the bed and settle my weight on Kara. My hands run gently over her body before setting on either side of her head.

"Kara, I need you so damn bad," I whisper against her mouth.

When her eyes open at my words, I slowly slide into her and connect our bodies the way our hearts are already connected.

We rock together, enjoying the passion that we share as our bodies seek out the ultimate crescendo. Looking into her eyes, I feel her warmth blanket me, putting me at peace and wrapping me up in a cocoon of her love. This right here is what it's all about folks. Being connected to someone.

Being part of them – mind, body and soul. It's hard to describe the utter feeling of rightness when it happens. It just is. And what it is, is perfection.

Only when her climax takes over, does Kara break eye contact. Her head falls back, and her eyes roll into her head. Her back and neck arches, and a low moan is stifled by her gag. Her whole body twitches and convulses with the force of her release. A few moments later, I join her and come deep inside her.

My forehead rests on hers, and I find myself panting, not from exertion but from the overwhelming need to crawl inside her and stay there forever.

Quickly undoing the cuffs and removing the gag, I then wrap Kara up in my arms and knead her arm muscles to get blood flowing back to them. Lying on the bed, our legs are wrapped around each other, and her head rests on my chest.

"I love you," she whispers and the corners of my mouth tip up into a grin.

"I love you too, Sunshine. Thank you for letting me do that. It's humbling how much you trust me."

"I could never not trust you, babe. Always."

I roll over her, pressing her back into the bed. "Marry me." The words leave my mouth before I even realize what I'm saying.

"I thought I was," Kara says with a look of confusion on her face.

A thought enters my brain, and at first I go to dismiss it, but then I think it just might be brilliant. Our families are going to be all together. Why not?

"No. I mean now. Soon. I want you to be my wife. Screw the big, fancy wedding. My family is here. Your parents are here. Let's get married right after Christmas." A huge smile takes over my face because the very thought that she will be my wife makes me downright giddy. And I don't care if that means a hit to my masculinity, because I am, in fact, bursting with giddiness right now.

"Okay."

"Okay?" I ask, wanting to make sure we are both on the same page.

"Yes. You know how much I hate being the center of attention. I just about ran out on Brad and Sophie's wedding. The last thing I'd want to do is leave you standing at the altar looking like a chump," she jokes, and I feign being insulted.

"A chump, huh?" I ask as my fingers dig into her sides. Her body wriggles and she snorts with laughter as I continue to tickle her.

"Okay, okay! I give! You are so not a chump!" She recalls her earlier statement and swats at my arm playfully.

"What am I then? A sex god? Your master? The most kick ass, awesome man you've ever laid eyes on?" I could go on and on, but really what's the point? I know I'm all those things to her already.

"Don't make me answer that." When I don't let her off the hook, she begs. "Please."

Her bottom lip sticks out in a pout and her eyes blink up at me endearingly. She knows that little innocent look of hers does me in every time. It's the best way for her to get whatever she wants out of me.

"Fine... So, we're doing this? In just a few days, you'll be Mrs. Jacob Matthews?" I ask, slightly stunned by the fact that this is actually happening, and I didn't even need to persuade her.

"Mrs. Jacob Matthews," she echoes with a wistful sigh. "It sounds perfect."

I kiss the tip of her nose and snuggle into her, like the big mush that she makes me. "That it does."

Chapter Seven

Sam

I walk triumphantly out of Toys 'R Us, pushing Tessa's stroller. I got the damn Elmo alright. I might have had to be a little underhanded to do it, but I got it. The bitch deserved it anyhow.

"You stole her Elmo?" Michelle asks in between laughs.

"Well, technically. When the clerk put the dolls on the shelf, the women there descended like vultures. I had to push Tessa towards the side so she didn't get hurt in the stampede and when I reached for the last one, that witch grabbed it from my hand." I cradle my cell phone between my chin and shoulder as I situate my packages in the stroller.

"Was it actually in your hands or was it still on the shelf?" Michelle asks with a serious tone to her voice.

"What difference does it make?" I reply, while walking down the strip mall towards the photography studio, where I parked my Tahoe. After I drop off these bags in the car, I need to pick up the last of Aiden's gifts.

"It makes a big difference actually. If it was off the shelf and fully in your hands, then she stole it from you. But if the box was still resting on the shelf and you both grabbed it at the same time, then it was 'may the best woman win' territory."

"I don't really know," I grumble, pissed that if what she says is true, then I probably shouldn't have chased the woman down and stolen the Elmo out of her cart when she wasn't looking.

"Oh my God! You are such a bitch! You stole that poor woman's Christmas present!" Michelle hoots into the phone, knowing full well what my silence says.

"I… I have to call you back…" My voice stutters and trails off as I hang up the phone on Michelle. It immediately starts ringing so I push the button to send her straight to voicemail.

I watch in astonishment as Jacob and a redheaded beauty walk hand-in-hand down the strip. His eyes are shining and happy as he tugs on her arm to stop her forward progression. He reaches up and tucks her hair behind her ear, before leaning down and brushing his lips against hers. The woman leans into him, placing her hand on his chest and curling her fingers into the lapel of his jacket.

My steps falter, and tears prick the back of my eyes. My heart begins to break at the sight of the two of them. It's not that I want Jacob for myself. I'm happy and in love with

Aiden. It's just a total shock to see him so obscenely happy. I don't think I've ever seen him look the way he does now, as I watch him whisper into her ear.

They start walking again, right towards me. But I'm still stuck in place, grieving over the loss of a love that it turns out, I never really had.

When I realize that there is nowhere for me to hide, I begin to panic. I don't know if I can handle seeing them together. The very thought of meeting this mystery woman, scares me.

It's been at least a year and a half since I saw Jacob last. I sent him away after learning about Aiden and Brooke's deceit, and the difference is night and day. I wanted him to find a woman who would make him happy, I just didn't realize that I never actually made him happy. Not even one iota as much as this person does. It's plain to see.

Jacob is visibly startled when he sees me standing in the middle of the sidewalk, staring. He looks worriedly at the redhead, before walking over to me.

"Hi, Sam. I'd like to introduce you to Kara," he says, wrapping his arm around Kara's waist. "Kara, this is Sam."

Kara gives me a tight lipped smile before extending her arm to shake my hand. I mentally note that she has a nice handshake. I can't stand women with limp handshakes.

"She's gotten big," Jacob notes, gesturing to Tessa in her stroller.

"She's almost two years old now. It feels like yesterday that she was placed in my arms for the first time," I say wistfully.

"Sam, is this your daughter?" Kara asks while giving Tessa a genuine smile.

"It is. Say hi, Tessa."

"Hi," Tessa's little voice squeaks out, and Kara bends her knees and squats in front of the stroller to talk to her.

"How are you?" Jacob's deep voice shakes my very core. I turn my attention to him, seeing how he is studying me intently.

"I'm really good. How are you?"

He glances at Kara with a soft look and then turns back to me. "I'm really good too."

"You look happy and settled," I say softly, trying to keep our conversation as quiet as possible.

He nods his head and gives me a small smile. His green eyes are soft and warm.

God, I've missed him. I wish things had gone differently between us and that we could have been friends.

"So how did you and Kara meet?" I ask when Kara stands back up and steps closer to Jacob's side.

"She was Brooke's friend actually." Jacob clears his throat and looks uncomfortably between the two of us. Hearing her name is like splashing me with cold water and bringing me back to reality. So many things I wish I could change.

How strange it must have been for them since she was Brooke's friend. I wonder how that whole thing came about. She doesn't look like she is as evil as Brooke. One look at Brooke and you would have sworn you were facing Medusa herself and feared that you would turn to stone. But Kara looks like she might have been an angel just sent down from heaven. Complete opposite to Brooke in every way.

"I'm really sorry about your friend," I offer my condolences to her. Even if I hate Brooke with a passion, Kara obviously would have cared about her.

Kara smiles back, and I'm mesmerized by how beautiful she is. If there was ever a doubt in my mind why Jacob would want to be with her, I wouldn't have it any longer after seeing her face unguarded.

"Thank you. I know this is awkward for all of us, but you have a beautiful daughter and I'm really glad that I finally got a chance to meet you," Kara says shyly and links her hand with Jacob's. It's clearly a show of support, and my heart squeezes for him. Instead of making this harder on him, she's trying to make it easier. He found someone to soothe him, and it is obvious that they are meant to be together.

"I'm so happy for the two of you…" My words die off when I notice the sparkler on her left hand. "And it looks like a congratulations is in order."

Kara looks at her hand and smiles. "Yes, thank you."

Jacob and her exchange a small, knowing look, and I feel the tears welling up in my eyes. I need to get out of here before these damn hormones take over, and I make a blubbering mess out of myself. I blink a few times to clear my eyes.

"I better get going. I have to finish picking some stuff up before Tessa's nap. It was really good to see you. Both of you," I finish with a smile of my own.

Jacob lets go of Kara's hand and reaches out to hug me. At first, I'm taken aback by his show of affection, but I quickly shake it off and hug him back. In the back of my mind, I know it must be hard for Kara to watch us, but this moment is truly about us saying goodbye to each other. It's us fully letting go of the past and all the mistakes that went along with it.

"Take care," he whispers in my ear, before stepping back and leading Kara away.

I stand on the sidewalk and watch them walk into a jewelry store, before hustling to my car. When I get to the car, I sag against the side and breathe deeply in an attempt to calm my riotous emotions. I'm so damn happy for Jacob, and I finally feel like that part of my life is where it should be.

$\mathcal{K}$ara

Walking into the jewelry store to pick out our wedding rings, Jacob puts his hand on my lower back and leads me to the counter.

"Good afternoon. What can I help you with?" The nice, older lady asks from behind the counter.

"We're looking for wedding bands," Jacob answers her, never taking his hand from my back. I'm not sure how he knows I need the contact, especially after seeing his ex, but I'm grateful that he does.

What are the chances we run into Samantha on our way to pick out wedding bands? Seriously.

"Anything in particular? Yellow gold, white gold, platinum, titanium?" The lady moves over to a display case, and we follow.

"Platinum for her and I guess titanium for me," Jacob shrugs. He is such a man. I know he doesn't care what goes on his finger as long as it's manly and doesn't turn his finger green. He told me so just last night after we decided to move up our wedding.

"Of course. Let me see your engagement ring, dear."

I hold my left hand out while she fingers the ring.

"I have a few ideas. If you don't mind waiting a few moments, I can pull together some rings for you two to look at."

We both agree and she scurries away, leaving us alone in the storeroom.

Jacob turns to me with concern in his eyes. I can see they are sharply focused and intently studying me. Sheesh. I'm not some weak flower that's going to wilt just because we saw Samantha. Sure, I could have gone the rest of my life without ever *actually* meeting her, but I'd be lying if I said I wasn't curious to see what she looked like and how the two of them would interact with each other.

"Are you okay with that whole scene back there?" He asks while gesturing towards the sidewalk outside.

"I'm fine. I wasn't lying when I said I was glad to finally get a chance to meet her. And her daughter is absolutely gorgeous."

"She is. I was afraid you were going to be upset seeing Sam. Especially given our history and what you thought about her and I before."

"Jacob, please. You don't need to worry about me. The past is in the past. You told me you were over her and I know you love me, so I'm good. We're good." I reassure him and wrap my arms around his waist.

"I do love you, Sunshine. You're it for me. My beginning and my ending." He reciprocates my hold and kisses me lightly on the mouth.

"Good. That's all I need to know. So, I'm assuming you're okay with the fact that *you* just saw Samantha?"

"More than okay, actually. Sometimes I still feel a little guilty about everything that happened between us. It was nice to see her and know that she's doing well. I feel like I can finally let the guilt go and know that she's going to have the future she deserves. Almost like closure."

"That's a good way to look at it."

The lady rejoins us at the counter with multiple black velvet ring holders and my breath catches at all the stunning rings. How the hell am I going to pick one?

We spend the next hour looking at each one. Jacob quickly picks out a simple, wide banded, silver tungsten carbide ring with beveled edges. I, on the other hand, am having serious issues deciding. I might not care about the big wedding with a frilly, frou frou gown and tons of flowers, but I do care about my wedding band. I always assumed that once I saw the one, I'd know it right away. But right now, I'm suffering from a major case of indecisiveness.

"Don't see the one you want?" Jacob finally asks after I've tried on what feels like a hundred rings.

I feel my emotions getting the better of me, when I turn to him with tear filled eyes. I shake my head and give him a sad smile. I feel bad making him stand here, but I can't make up my mind and this is too big of a decision to not be sure. It's a lot of pressure.

"Hey. Don't worry about it. We'll find you the one." He pulls me in for a comforting hug and kisses my hair.

"We're getting married in just a few days. I have to pick one," I practically whine into his chest.

Jacob loosens his hold on me and turns to the lady, still keeping me tucked into his side.

"Do you have any other ones we can look at?"

"We do, sir. I have one that I think would be perfect for her, but it's rather expensive," she replies, referring to the price range we originally gave her.

"No. That's quite alright," I say quickly.

"Price isn't a factor," Jacob speaks at the same time.

The lady looks at us, unsure of which one of us she should listen to.

"I'll just pick one of these," I speak up.

"You will not. Kara, I want you to have the perfect ring. I don't care how much it costs. You're worth it. This ring is going to sit on your finger for the rest of your life. It has to be perfect. No ifs and or buts about it." He looks back at the lady and says, "Please go get us more to look at."

God, he's so wonderful.

"I hate the thought of you spending too much money on this," I grumble under my breath.

"What good is money if I can't spend it on you and, sooner rather than later, our kids? Now stop complaining."

I guess that conversation is closed.

The woman returns with one ring and the world seems to stop when I pick it up to look at it. I have tunnel vision right now.

The antique band is contoured to fit with a ring similar to mine. It's set with pave diamonds and sapphires and is breathtaking. Surprisingly, it is the perfect complement to my engagement ring. I didn't think that was possible.

"Gorgeous isn't it?" The woman asks as I slip the ring on my finger along with my engagement ring.

"It is," I breathe. Holding my hand out and watching the way the gems catch and reflect the light is mesmerizing. I feel like I've died and gone to heaven.

"How much is it?" I ask even though I don't want to know. The sensible side of me will be far too disappointed once I know the price tag.

When she tells us, my stomach hits the floor. Ho-ly shit!

"You can't spend that on my ring, Jacob."

"I sure as hell can. If you could have seen the look on your face when you first saw it, you'd know that I wouldn't have it any other way." He turns and faces the woman. "We'll take it."

Even though I know that this is too much, I'm beyond thrilled inside that I'm getting my dream ring.

I reluctantly remove the new ring from my finger and hand it over. Only a few more days before I can stare at it all the time.

Chapter Eight

Sam

"It was so surreal seeing him again," I say to my best friend, Michelle, as we sip tea and leaf through bridal magazines.

Michelle is finally getting married. I say finally because she hunted for "Mr. Right" for so long that I wasn't sure she even knew exactly what she was looking for. Then along came Kyle. He is just the sweetest, and he looks at her like she is the next best thing since sliced bread. He has brown hair that he wears buzzed and muscles that go on for days. His ruggedness goes well with my friend's classic Marilyn Monroe look.

Kyle is an ex-Army Ranger, who currently works construction. Once Michelle and him hooked up, Aiden got Kyle a great job working under one of the top contractors that his firm uses. I love having her with someone who gets along so well with Aiden.

"Seeing who again?" Aiden asks as he comes into the kitchen, catching the tail end of our conversation.

"Sam saw Jacob when she was shopping yesterday," Michelle blurts out, and I kick her under the table. I so didn't want Aiden to know what happened. With the bullshit going on with Rocky, I wasn't comfortable dragging those skeletons out of the closet. I felt it was best to let it go.

Fucking Michelle.

"Oh really?" Aiden quirks his eyebrow and gives me a censured look. I knew he wouldn't be happy about my seeing Jacob, which is why I didn't tell him about Jacob approaching me in the park that day over a year ago either. Nothing good can come out of throwing salt into an open wound, and I fear Jacob will be just that to Aiden for a long time.

"Yeah, he was with his fiancée," she throws in for good measure. Apparently, I didn't kick her hard enough.

I give her a scathing look. She glances back at me with a "What?" look.

"It was nothing really," I play it off. "They were shopping and we bumped into each other. He introduced us and we talked for a minute before saying goodbye. Like I said, it was nothing at all."

Aiden lifts a fresh bottle of beer to his lips, before taking a few slugs. He sets it down on the counter a little too harshly, and I cringe inside at the fallout that will ensue for keeping this from him.

"Well isn't that just great," he says sarcastically before grabbing a bag of chips and joining Kyle in the family room to watch football.

"What the hell were you thinking?" I whisper nastily at Michelle once he leaves the room.

"What? I thought you guys didn't hide anything from each other?"

"We don't, but I haven't told him about Jacob because I didn't want to upset him. Besides, it's a little too close to home with the fighting we've been doing about that Rocky chick lately."

"Fuck. I didn't think of that. Has anything else happened since he spent his day off with her working on a 'design issue'?" She makes the air quotes around design issue and my heart crumbles. Even I know the reason he left sounds kind of lame. Especially since he was gone for so long.

"Just a bunch of phone calls. She actually called at like ten o'clock a couple of nights ago. She wanted to double check that he remembered their early morning meeting the next day." I give her a look of disbelief and fist my hands on the table. That quick little reminder of hers took up a twenty minute phone call.

"Either your husband is oblivious to her true intentions or he's enjoying it. I don't know what to tell you." Michelle sits back and picks up her coffee mug. She gives me a sad look over the rim.

"I know," I sigh in defeat. "All I can do is see how this will play out. As far as I know they haven't done anything inappropriate together. I just pray he doesn't end up making the same mistakes I did. I'm not sure we can come back from that." This is the first time I've said my true worry out loud. Until now, I avoided it, afraid that it would come true if I verbalized it.

"It will be okay. Have faith in your marriage and trust Aiden to do the right thing." She grabs my hand and offers me silent support.

"So what do you think of this dress for your daughter at the wedding?" Michelle holds up a magazine photo of a white, silk tulle tiered dress. It's a sleeveless number with delicate ribbon trimmed tulle layers with a beautiful bow and sash to finish it off.

"You sure you want her to wear white?" I ask, secretly thankful she changed the subject.

"Yeah. I don't see why not. She's not just the flower girl, she's my goddaughter. She should stand out." Michelle waves me off like I'm crazy.

"Okay…." I stand up and grab another cup of tea.

"Can you believe we're actually planning my wedding? This is so exciting. I'm just so damn happy!" My friend exclaims.

I walk over and give her a big hug. "I know honey. I can't wait."

What I fail to tell her is that her wedding is coming at a potentially bad time for me. I'll wait to burst that bubble.

Right now this needs to be about her and her future with Kyle.

A little while later, Aiden joins us in the kitchen, and he puts their empty beer bottles on the counter. "I just got a call from Rocky. Seems some big investors are coming into town tomorrow, so don't plan dinner around me. I'll probably have to take them out for dinner and drinks afterward."

Well, isn't that convenient. I look over at Michelle, and she gives me a knowing look.

"Sure thing, Aiden," I murmur and flip the page of the magazine in front of me a little harder than I needed to.

Tension and stress is so not good for me right now. I wish there was some way I could make this bitch go away.

Aiden

"Glad you guys could make it today," I say while shaking Mr. Klein's hand.

"Pleasure was ours, Aiden. Sorry we can't join you for drinks, but we need to get on the road." The short, stocky man says. His face is red and round. He kind of reminds me of Santa, but without the beard.

"We'll keep the offer open for next time," Rocky replies and shakes the man's hand along with his two associates.

Once they are out the door, she turns to me with a smile. "Just because they couldn't have a drink, doesn't mean we can't."

I watch as she walks down the hall towards my office. I always keep some scotch in a crystal decanter that Sam gave me when I got promoted and I know that's what she is heading for. As she walks away, I can't help but notice the sway of her hips in that tight, black dress of hers.

I shake my head and silently chastise myself. That is one thing I should *not* be noticing.

Inside my office, I find Rocky perched on the ledge of my desk, the way she usually does. Her left foot is propped on one of the chairs in front of the desk. Her dress has ridden up her legs, and I can see the tops of her stockings where they attach to her garter belt. I swallow hard and turn my attention away from her.

"I should probably get going. I usually like to get home before Tessa goes to bed." I start putting papers in my briefcase, hoping she'll get the hint.

Ever since Sam brought up her unease with Rocky, I've started to notice that maybe the woman isn't really as friendly as I initially thought. She seems to have a way of clinging to me and a couple of the other guys in the office. Ben and I had a conversation about it just yesterday. He wasn't too keen on her either. Said she made him uncomfortable and if his wife ever saw the way she acted, she'd probably rip her eyes out.

Women… can't they just trust us not to stick our dicks where they don't belong?

"Oh, come on. Just one drink isn't going to hurt anything. You'll be home before she goes down." Rocky gets up and walks over to the decanter and pours us each a glass. She slinks over to me like a cat after her prey, handing me a glass.

Well, Sam did meet up with her ex just the other day and failed to tell me about it. Having a drink with Rocky might not be that bad. It's not like her and I are having an affair. One drink… I can handle one drink. I just wish we weren't the only ones in the office right now. The room is starting to feel hot, and I stop myself from pulling on my collar in uneasiness.

"So… the meeting went well tonight. You were amazing with them. I like watching you in action. You're so strong and sure of yourself. I find confidence very appealing in a man." Her red painted nail runs down the length of my tie and stops just above my belt buckle. I take a step back and set my glass down.

"What's the matter?" She asks, moving closer to me again.

"Nothing. I just really need to get home." I start to slide out from between her and the desk, but she moves back into my way.

"Aiden… I don't bite. Not unless you want me to," she whispers and runs her hands up my arm, squeezing my biceps. "So tell me, is that what you want?"

Before I can answer her, her mouth covers mine, and she pulls my body flush with hers. I wrap my hands around her waist and start to move her back, but she latches on and wraps her leg around my hip, grinding against me.

Her tongue runs along my jaw to my ear. "I know you want me."

I push her away forcefully and wipe my mouth.

"What do you think you're doing?" I ask with disgust.

Rocky laughs and lowers the zipper on her dress, letting it fall to the floor. She stands before me in a black lace bra and her garter and stockings. Apparently, she likes to go commando.

"Aiden, I just want to make you feel good. And in turn, I want you to make me feel good. I'm wet just thinking about you. Want to see?" She sits back on my desk and spreads her legs wide. I quickly close my eyes and turn away.

"You're delusional is what you are. Put this back on." I pick up her dress and throw it at her. Instead, she just laughs and tosses it aside. When I chance a look back at her, she's actually masturbating on my desk. Is this some sort of sick dream? Am I being punked?

"Oh my God," she gasps and inserts a finger inside herself. "I can just imagine what you would feel like. Aiden, please come make me feel good. I've seen you look at me. I know you've thought about me. Why else would you always spend time with me and talk to me on the phone. You want me."

"Will you stop that already? I don't want you. Why would I throw my perfectly good life away just to fuck you?" I grab my briefcase and make to leave. Maybe now she'll get the hint.

She moans, and I glance down at her hand which is covered in the evidence of her arousal. My cock starts to stir at the sight. Shit. I hate when it has a mind of its own.

"I don't want you to leave your life. I just want you to fuck me, right here on this desk. I want it hard and I want it dirty. I'll even let you choose how we do it. I don't really care as long as you fuck me already. Show me what a man you are." She taunts me as she continues to pleasure herself. My eyes can't seem to look away from what she's doing.

In and out followed by little circles. And repeat. I feel like I'm in a trance staring at her. Sam's face suddenly floats into my mind, and I snap myself out of it. This is wrong on so many levels.

"I'll be reporting this to McGee in the morning. Lock up on the way out." I practically run for the door and out of the office.

At the first stop light I encounter, I put my head on the steering wheel and take a deep breath. Holy shit that bitch is whacked. I could understand how a weaker man would have succumbed to her. I wouldn't be surprised if she's done that a hundred times before and was met with exactly the type of behavior she was hoping for.

I pick up my cell phone and dial home. When Sam picks up, guilt twists in my chest.

"Hey, honey. Just wanted you to know that my night ended earlier than I thought. I should be home in time to give Tessa her bath." I will my voice to stay steady and not give anything away.

"That's great news. I'll hold off until you get here then. I love you."

"I love you too," I reply before hanging up.

When the light turns green, I punch the gas and put that horrible scene behind me.

Chapter Nine

Jacob

Pulling into Emma's driveway, I breathe a sigh of relief. The snow is really coming down now, and the roads were horrible once we hit Pennsylvania.

Bill and Maggie pull in behind us and step out of their car. Thankfully, they will be leaving the day after we get married to give us some time alone. I think they were planning on staying longer until we informed them of our plans to move the wedding up. I mentally shudder at the thought of having to curb our sexual activities any longer. The other night with the handcuffs was nice… beyond nice actually, but I doubt Kara would let me do that all the time.

Our wedding is all set up thanks to the help of Maggie and Emma. Maggie took Kara shopping for a dress, while Emma arranged for her minister to marry us in her living room the day after Christmas. Brad and Sophie will be joining us as long as Sophie doesn't pop between now and then. I tried to tell them it wasn't necessary that they attend, but Sophie insisted. Mack is going to drive up as well to support us. Our wedding will be just what it should be, a small affair with close family and friends. Nothing more.

Our honeymoon is another story. Seeing as how we weren't anticipating getting hitched over Christmas, I can't get the time off from work. We decided to go somewhere warm for Valentine's Day. I'm thinking the Dominican Republic. I've heard great things about the resorts, and it will be nice and warm there, when it's good and cold here. Plus it comes with the added benefit of keeping Kara in a bikini for the whole trip.

I mentally fist pump the air thinking how in less than forty-eight hours, Kara will be tied to me forever. It can't come soon enough for me.

After we are all out of the cars, we drag our suitcases inside through the garage. Once in the mud room, we proceed to shake the snow off of ourselves.

"Uncle Jacob! Aunt Kara!" Grace and Candace run into the room, full of excitement and cry out a little too loudly in my opinion.

"Hey, munchkins!" I pick each one up and kiss their cheeks before setting them down and letting them maul Kara.

"Hi, baby brother!" Emma greets us warmly as we step into the kitchen. "You must be Kara's parents. I'm Jacob's sister, Emma. And these rugrats are Candace and Grace."

"Pleased to meet you, Emma. You have a lovely home," Bill says shaking her hand.

"And your daughters are beautiful. Thank you so much for letting us spend the holiday with you," Maggie adds as she hugs Emma.

"Thank you. It's my pleasure to have you here. Please come in and I'll show everyone to their rooms," Emma replies, then proceeds to quickly and efficiently lead us to our designated rooms.

Kara's parents are staying in the guest room while Kara and I are staying on the new pullout couch in John's basement man cave. Thankfully, Kara and I won't have to squeeze into Grace's bed this time around, and we'll have the added benefit of some privacy. *Hint, hint.*

"Where's John?" I ask as we all gather in the living room with eggnog, while the movie *Elf* plays on the television.

"He's working late, trying to finish a few things up before his long weekend. He'll be home before the girls go to bed," Emma replies with a frown on her face. I make a mental note to talk to her about that later. I know John works crazy hours, and I wonder if it is starting to weigh on my sister. Sometimes I wish I lived closer so that she had more help when he was out of town or working late. It can't be easy not having family close by when you have kids. When Kara and I have children, I want that type of support system for us.

"What did you ask Santa for?" Kara asks the girls some time later.

"I want Santa to bring me Monster High dolls, Barbie's, jewelry like you Aunt Kara, a new American Girl doll and makeup. Oh and an iPad," Grace spouts off her list in a fast ramble.

"You're too young for makeup," Emma lectures Grace from the kitchen, proving she can hear just about anything regardless of her location.

"I want an iPad, jewelry, a new iPod because Grace broke mine…"

"I did not!" Grace argues animatedly with Candace.

"You did too!" Candace yells back.

"Did not!"

"Did too! Mom!" I feel like I'm watching a tennis tournament as our heads go back and forth between the two girls arguing.

"Girls! That's enough! We have company." Emma stands in the doorway with her hands on her hips. One look at her and the girls immediately stop fighting.

"I want a puppy too." Candace goes back to naming the things she wants for Christmas.

"Oh yeah! I want a puppy too! Uncle Jacob you should see the puppies! They are so cute!" Grace jumps up and down.

Thank God I got them those dogs. Yet again I'll have the best present this year.

"Puppies, huh? Don't you think you're a little too young for one?" I tease them, knowing I'm about to get them yelled at again.

"We are not too young!" Candace stomps her feet and crosses her arms.

"Yeah! I'm eight years old!" Grace snaps at me.

"Nope, I think you are still too young. Sorry girls. I'm going to have to call Santa and tell him he most definitely should *not* bring you a puppy." I sit back in my chair and cross my legs, resting my ankle on my knee, feeling pretty smug with myself.

"Noooooo!" Candace calls out at the same time Grace starts crying.

I lose my smugness when a hand slaps me on the back of the head.

"Hey," I say and turn in my chair to see a very pissed off Emma standing behind me. If looks could kill, I'd surely be dead right now.

"Sorry," I grumble and rub my smarting head.

Kara shakes her head mockingly at me and gives me a "What were you thinking?" look.

"Hey, Bill. What do you say we head downstairs and see if we can catch a game of some sort?" I say, wanting to step out of the lion's den.

"Lead the way," he replies with a big smile and follows me down to the basement.

There weren't any games on seeing as how it's Christmas Eve, but Bill and I are having no trouble at all watching ESPN for our sports fix.

Hearing footsteps on the stairs, I turn my head and spy Kara coming down to join us.

"Hey, Sunshine. Got tired of being with the girls?" I ask when she sits on my lap. For as much as I love the feel of her pressed to my groin, I'm immediately suspicious that she is being this affectionate in front of her father.

"No. I was hoping you'd do me a favor," she says sweetly as she blinks up at me with that innocent looking expression that always does me in.

I groan in response, knowing this spells trouble for me.

"Do I even want to know?" I deadpan.

"Well see, a neighbor was supposed to stop over tonight dressed as Santa since Candace is at that age where she's wavering on whether he is real or not. Anyways, Emma is afraid she's going to ruin it for Grace, so she thought this would be a good idea. Only, the guy had something come up last minute and can't do it. He offered us use of his suit though."

And there is the heart of what she wants. Shit. I don't want to dress up as jolly, old Saint Nick. But then a light bulb goes off in my head.

"Well that's easy. Who cares if he can't do it? Emma can find another way to convince the girls that he is real." I mentally pat myself on the back for getting out of that one.

"I could see where you'd think that would be an easy solution, but the girls already know Santa is coming. How would they feel if Santa suddenly canceled? It would be counterproductive really." She gives me those damn eyes again, and I know I'm not getting out of this unscathed.

"Why can't their father do it?" I grasp at my last hope for getting out of dress up time.

"Emma said he sprained his wrist the other day, so the girls would know it wasn't really Santa once they saw the brace."

"Damn it," I mumble under my breath.

Kara leans in and whispers in my ear, "I promise I'll make it worth your while."

Her words coupled with the feel of her breath on my skin, has my cock stirring. *Down boy… Santa cannot sport wood.*

"Fine. Bring me the damn suit," I grumble begrudgingly.

"You're the best! You know that?" Kara kisses me chastely. Her father is still there after all.

Bill laughs once Kara bolts up the stairs.

"Laugh now. Next thing you know she'll make you be my elf!" I threaten good naturedly.

"I'd love to see that," he says in between chuckles.

"Ah crap!" I pull my hands through my hair, seriously wanting to throw a child-sized temper tantrum at this turn of events.

"Think of it this way, son. It will be good practice for when you have kids. And you're making those girls' night."

"Yeah… alright. I guess I can try to look on the bright side of things," I concede. The last thing I need is for my soon to be father-in-law to think I'm a big baby.

Kara returns twenty minutes later with a giant red bag. I drag it into the bathroom and take my time changing. Part of me hopes that if I take too long the girls will fall asleep or something. Stranger things have happened.

"It's Christmas Eve, Jacob. The girls won't want to fall asleep regardless, so don't think you can get out of this," Kara calls through the door.

How the hell does she do that? It's worse than the eyes in the back of her head.

"I'll be out in a minute," I yell through the door.

After I velcro the giant pillow onto my belly, I turn to the side and stick my stomach out further, poking at my now enlarged gut. I roll my abdominal muscles making the pillow bounce and ripple. Chuckling at my nonsense, I step into the red, velvet pants. I pull the black suspenders over my shoulder and do a little jig watching as my stomach bounces around.

Apparently, this suit sucks the seriousness out of you. *Maybe it's a magic suit…*

I stop my musings and proceed to put the jacket on and button it up.

I look damn good in red. Even with a giant stomach.

Next comes the wig and beard, followed by the hat. Now I have absolutely no reason to not walk out of this bathroom. Damn.

Opening the door, Kara is the first thing I see. Her face lights up and she graces me with a wide smile. She lifts her arm, and then she does the unthinkable when she snaps a picture with her cell phone.

"Lump of coal for you!" I shout and make like I'm going to attack her. When I lunge for her, she screeches and runs across the room.

Once I catch up with her, she reaches out and rubs red shit on my cheeks.

"Really?" I ask not wanting to deal with this shit.

"You are so going to get lucky later," she mumbles so only I can hear her.

"Damn straight. You owe me one creative session, Sunshine."

"There is this new position I heard about that I've been curious to try."

"It's a good thing this suit is big, otherwise my sister would think Santa was a giant perv. What do you think you're doing telling me that now?" I gripe, knowing my nieces can't sit on my lap while I'm turned on.

"Sorry. I forget," she says like that explains it all.

"You're lucky I love you." I kiss her cheek and start towards the stairs. "Let's get this over with."

"That position is pretty damn amazing if I do say so myself," Kara informs me in between pants. Like I didn't already know she came harder than I've ever felt her come before.

"I think my head blew off with the force of my release," I concur with her observation. "That position just went on the short list."

After we finally catch our breaths, we snuggle up together and my fingers play with the curls in her hair. My body is fully sated from our first uninhibited bout of love making since her parents came to visit a week ago.

"You're a good uncle, wearing that suit for the girls. And I know for a fact Emma appreciated it. I saw her wiping tears from her eyes," Kara says after several long minutes.

"What's up with her anyway? Has she said anything to you?" I ask, remembering that I wanted to talk to Emma about how upset she looked earlier.

I feel Kara's shoulder shrug before she answers me. "Nothing much. I think she might just be depressed."

"Depressed, huh? I wonder why?" I ponder the reasons it could be while trying to think of anything she might have said to me during recent conversations.

"John is supposed to go to Germany for like a month after New Years. I think his job is starting to get to her."

Sometimes I wish John would take a job that doesn't involve so much travel. I know he loves his wife and kids, so I'm not sure why he doesn't feel driven to stay. To find a job that won't always take him away from them.

"I'll talk to her tomorrow." I kiss Kara's head and gather her tighter in my arms. I always look forward to our pillow talk.

My cell phone buzzes on the end table, so I reach over to pick it up. The bright light from the screen, against the darkness in the room, momentarily hurts my eyes.

"Sophie just had her baby." My face breaks into a smile as I read the text Brad sent. A glance at the clock tells me it's after midnight, which means they have a Christmas baby.

"Oh my God! What did they name it?" Kara jumps up and makes a grab for my phone. I hold it away from her, forcing her to get close and look over my shoulder to see the message.

Brad and Sophie held the name of their firstborn close to their vest. No one knew, not even their parents.

"Duncan Jacob McGuire. He was seven pounds, nine ounces and twenty-one inches long. Awwww! They named him after you." I watch as she wipes a tear from the corner of her eye after reading the rest of the message out loud.

"Imagine that? That's pretty damn cool." Okay… it's extremely cool, but I'm trying to keep my ego in check here.

"It is." Kara sets my phone back on the table and curls up in my arms again. We lay in silence a little while longer.

I'm just about to recommend we try and get some sleep when she interrupts me.

"Jacob…" Her voice trails off and I look down to see her biting her lip.

"What's up, Sunshine?" I say, curious about what's bugging her. She only bites her lip when she's upset or nervous.

"There's something I want to talk to you about, but I'm not sure how."

"You can tell me anything, Kara. You know that." I kiss the top of her head and squeeze her reassuringly.

"It's just… this is a delicate subject and I don't want to freak you out." Leading with that statement is a sure fire way to get someone to freak out. Someone less level-headed than me of course.

"I promise I won't freak out." I realize this is a promise that will be hard to keep depending on what she says, but for her I'll try.

"I want a baby," she blurts out after several minutes and then slaps her hand on her forehead. "I should have eased you into that."

I barely hear her words. My body is frozen in its spot. A baby?

"Where did that come from?" I finally ask, trying to keep my tone light.

"Sorry, I didn't mean to just throw it out there. I've felt this way for a while. My biological clock is ticking pretty damn hard. I just haven't wanted to say anything before now because we weren't getting married for a while…"

"And now that we're getting married tomorrow, you wanted to discuss it?" I finish for her.

"Yes."

I always knew I wanted kids with Kara. There was never a question about that. The real decision needs to be do I want them now? Am I ready for them now? Kara and I have only known each other for three years and half of that time we weren't even together. Maybe a little more time being able to travel whenever we want and make love whenever we want wouldn't be such a bad thing. Once you have kids you live for them. Gone are the days of sleeping in late and doing whatever you want.

However, the thought of Kara pregnant with my child makes it feel like a fire has been lit inside my chest. Warmth radiates out, and my heart feels light. I can just picture a little redheaded girl curled up on my lap while we watch the Red Sox play or a dark haired boy playing catch with me in the backyard.

Instead of answering her, I decide to sing in a low voice into her. I'm not sure where it comes from, the words just come out unexpectedly.

"Having my baby. What a wonderful way of saying how much you love me…"

When I finish, Kara looks up at me and it's easy to see that my words have made her ecstatic. "Are you saying you want a baby? Cause if you want to have more time with just the two of us, I'd understand."

"I want nothing more than to make a baby with you." I roll on top of her and kiss down her neck.

"What are you doing?" Her words come out breathy as my tongue circles her nipple.

"Practicing," I murmur around her breast. "Tomorrow, flush your pills."

A moan followed by her agreement comes, and we spend the next hour practicing our baby making skills.

Chapter Ten

Aiden

The traffic was ridiculous today. I should have known better than to wait until the last minute to pick up Sam's custom made gift. With work being a zoo right now, I just didn't find enough time.

Rocky was fired after I informed McGee of her less that businesslike behavior. The old man was actually proud of me for turning her down. Seems he has a soft spot for Sam.

I still haven't told her about the Rocky situation. All she knows is that Rocky is gone, and I'm picking up the slack. The last thing I need is to worry her any more than she already was.

At least I was smart enough to order Sam's gift months ago. Otherwise, I'd be royally screwed trying to find the time to pick something out for her. This gift is going to be perfect on her. There is no way she won't love it. I've made it my mission to give her thoughtful gifts the last few years. I want her to know how much I cherish her. There was a time when she questioned that fact, and I don't ever want to go back to those dark days.

By the time I get home, dinner has been served and Tessa is on her way to bed. I can't stand the thought that I missed playing with her tonight. Our daddy-daughter time is one of the highlights of my day. There is nothing more rewarding than having your child look at you like you are their everything. Tessa thinks I hang the moon, and I think she does, so the affection and adoration is mutual. She is my little girl for sure.

After reheating a plate of lasagna and eating it while standing in the kitchen, I collapse on the couch and pick up the latest thriller that I've been reading. Sam is sitting cross-legged on the floor, wrapping the gifts that still need to go under the tree. She insisted that Tessa wake up in the morning to gifts galore from Santa. My wife is nuts, but then again, I wouldn't have her any other way. Whatever it takes to make her happy I'm okay with.

A few hours later, my cock is straining against my zipper. I've been covertly looking at her ass all night when she thinks I'm reading. Every time she bends over to put a gift under the tree, the throbbing gets worse. Her ass looks spectacular in the black yoga pants she is wearing. They're tight and highlight every one of her God given curves. I want to set my hands on her hips and drive into her over and over when she's bent over like that. Even after all these years, Sam still gets my blood flowing.

I think a little Christmas Eve nookie is in order. I can't think of a better way to erase the stress from my last minute shopping.

When the last gift is placed carefully under the tree, I grab the mistletoe hanging in the doorway to the family room and make my way to Sam on the floor. Kneeling in front of her, I hold it over our heads and watch as her face breaks out into a bright smile. I lean over and brush my lips against hers. It's a brief touch meant to tease. When I pull back, I see her eyes are still closed, and her dreamy smile is back in place.

My hand slowly lifts up and my thumb lightly grazes her nipple, making her gasp. My mouth covers hers again, and I hold nothing back. This kiss is filled with longing and need. I need nothing more than to be inside her and feel her warmth surrounding me.

My hands skim over her collarbone, pushing her chunky button-up sweater off her shoulders and down her arms until it lands on the floor. My lips trail down her neck, and across her chest while my hands slip her tank top down her arms, revealing her bare breasts. Her nipples are pebbled and begging for my attention. I capture one between my lips and suck roughly, eliciting a moan from Sam. Her hands lock onto either side of my head, holding me in place while I alternately bite her nipple and lavish it with my tongue.

"My God, you have me so turned on Aiden," Sam says in between moans. "I need you inside me, honey. Now."

"Soon," I murmur against her breast. My fingers hook in her pants and draw them down her legs along with her red, satin underwear.

Sam leans back on the rug and watches as I part her folds and drag my finger through her wetness. "You're so wet, honey."

I watch as her face contorts in pleasure. The lights from the Christmas tree dance across her smooth skin, illuminating her like an angel. There is no way in hell I would have ever chanced ruining my relationship with Sam for Rocky. She has nothing on my wife.

Sam's head falls back, elongating her neck, when I start circling her tight little nub. I drag my mouth over the exposed skin of her neck, nibbling lightly.

Sam reaches out and pushes her hand under the waist of my pants and wraps it around my aching cock. Her movements are limited by the lack of space, so I use my free hand to pop my button and lower my zipper. Her hand works faster and pumps a little harder now that she can move a little easier, but it still isn't enough. I stop working her clit long enough to rid myself of my clothes.

Sam lies on the rug, while I kneel next to her. Her hand strokes my dick, while my fingers go back to work between her legs.

My breathing is becoming choppy, and I can feel my balls starting to tighten when her fist clamps a little tighter around my length. I insert two fingers into her slick channel and move them in and out while my thumb rubs against her clit. Her hips rise and work against my movements. It's hot as hell watching her fuck my hand right now.

I have to clench my teeth and fight the urge to come when her body stiffens and she cries out with her climax.

"I want to ride you," Sam pants out as her muscles continue to squeeze my fingers that are still inside her, prolonging her orgasm.

"You won't get any complaints from me," I respond while positioning myself next to her on the floor.

She looks like a goddess as she straddles my lap and lowers herself down over my length. I love watching myself disappear inside her and the way her flesh gives way. My hands still her once she's fully seated, so that I can savor the feeling of being wrapped up in her hot, wet silk.

"Show me what you got, honey," I coax her when I drop my hands and lean back on them to support myself.

Her sexy, smirk tells me that's just what she has in mind.

She starts out slow, circling her hips and rocking on me. Once she finds her rhythm, I use my hands behind me as leverage to thrust under her as she rides me hard and fast. With each movement, the rug rubs against my ass.

We move in perfect unison with each other, nearing the edge of bliss. I could look up at her forever. Her eyes gaze into mine and reflect back the passion that I have for her.

"So… good. So… damn… good," Sam stutters as she kneads her breasts and pinches her nipples. The movement draws my attention back to her tits. I lean my head forward and latch my mouth onto her right breast and suck hard, enjoying how good it feels when she grinds on me harder.

"Shit. I'm so sensitive. God, Aiden. Just like that," she says when my tongue flicks over her hardened nipple.

Before long, my balls are hard and tight. My release is imminent, and I'm not sure how much longer I'm going to be able to hold back. Her sheath feels like heaven right now as we continue to rock back and forth in harmony.

"Oh God. Oh God. Oh God," Sam chants when her orgasm hits. I thrust up a few more times, before coming long and hard inside her.

I collapse back on the floor and she slumps down over me as we work to even out our breathing. I lightly trail my fingers over her back, making her shiver.

"I'm going to have rug burns on my ass tomorrow," I say dryly. Sam laughs and her inner muscles clamp down rhythmically on my cock, which is still inside her. I groan at the over stimulation and carefully slide out of her. She rolls off me, onto her side, and rests her head on my chest.

"Sorry about that. At least your battle wounds will be worth it," she whispers as she places a gentle kiss on my chest.

"More than worth it," I respond with conviction.

We continue to lie next to the tree, staring up at the lights for a long while before Sam starts to get up.

"I don't want you to get up," I grouse as she raises the straps on her tank top and proceeds to grab our discarded clothing.

"Tessa will be up in like five hours. I don't know about you, but I could use some sleep." She tosses my clothes at me, and I deftly catch them.

"You're probably right. It's going to be a long day tomorrow between presents and going to see my family." I pull on my boxer briefs, turn off the lights and follow Sam up to our bedroom. Once we are both cleaned up and lying in bed, she snuggles close, and I smile into the darkness. My body is fully sated from making love to my amazing wife.

I have everything I need in life. Thank God no one has been able to successfully come between that so far.

Sam

"Mommy! Wanna see Santa!"

I groan and roll over at the sound of my overly excited child coming through the baby monitor. Thank God she's still in a crib. We agreed to transition her to a toddler bed next year, and I'm thankful that I can take a few moments to wake up before being forced to get out of bed.

I'm so damn tired. I may have gone a bit overboard with all the gifts for Tessa. Especially since I didn't take into account the fact that I had to wrap them all. Aiden is the worst wrapper known to mankind, so I don't even bother to ask him anymore. Given my current condition, I probably should have wrapped in small batches over the last week rather than doing a marathon wrap session last night.

Of course if Aiden hadn't jumped me under the tree, I would have had more sleep. I can feel myself heating at the memory of how good it felt to be with him last night. My hand drifts down to my belly and makes light circles around the waist of my pajama bottoms.

Speaking of Aiden...

I feel the heat of him on my back. His lips kiss the nape of my neck, and I roll over into his embrace. His kiss is light and sweet this morning.

"Merry Christmas," he murmurs against my lips.

"Merry Christmas," I whisper back before giving him a deep, wet kiss.

"Mommy! Daddy! Pwease come pway!" Tessa interrupts our make out session and we both groan in unison.

"I'll get her. You go ahead and shower while I make a quick breakfast," Aiden says before planting one last kiss on me and walking down the hall to Tessa's room.

"Don't let her open her stocking until I'm downstairs!" I call out to his retreating back.

My shower breathes some life back into me, but all I can think about is how I'm going to finagle a nap before heading to my mother-in-law's house. I don't want to miss a single moment of Christmas Day with Tessa. Last year, she was so small and the highlight of the day was watching her tiny, little fingers rip through the wrapping paper. She had no idea what she was opening. The excitement was more on my end, getting to see all the toys and clothes everyone got her. This year I've been reading her stories about Santa, and she can better appreciate receiving gifts.

I dress in a pair of worn, loose jeans, a white tank top and a red off-the-shoulder sweater, before heading downstairs. I can hear the sounds of bacon sizzling and Tessa playing with our St. Bernard, Hugo. Her little giggles are infectious and make my heart squeeze with love for my child. It never gets old hearing her laughter.

As I round the corner to the kitchen, I'm met with the force of a toddler running into my legs. I bend down and scoop up my little princess. She wraps her arms around my neck and gifts me with a tender kiss.

"Santa came!" She speaks enthusiastically.

"I know, baby! Did Daddy give you your stocking?" I ask while I set her in her booster seat at the kitchen table.

"Uh huh. Daddy said wait." She smiles and kicks her legs back and forth. She looks absolutely adorable in her pale pink pajama set with red snowflakes. But the pièce de résistance is her tiny, pale pink sweater slippers. They have fur trim with tiny white bows, and they are adorable. I love having a human doll to dress.

"Here, baby. While Daddy finishes your eggs, you can open your stocking." I hand the overflowing stocking to her, and she proceeds to rip through everything at top speed. I'm not even sure she is paying attention to everything as she rips the stocking open as fast as her little fingers will allow.

"You do realize that next year won't be this easy," I say wistfully to Aiden as he sets a plate of eggs in front of both me and Tessa. "Once she gets a better grip on the whole Santa thing, we'll be up at the crack of dawn racing down to the tree."

"Let's enjoy it while we can," he chuckles and joins us at the table. "Tessa, hurry up and eat so we can go open your presents."

I pick at my food while watching Aiden. His tight, white undershirt stretches nicely over his chest and arms. My man might not play football anymore, but he still has the body for it. Just remembering our heated session of love making last night has my body warming and me squirming in my seat.

Aiden clears his throat and draws my attention to his face. I feel the blush creep across my face, knowing I was caught staring. He gifts me with a gorgeous, mischievous grin.

"Ready mom?" He asks before picking up a squirming and giggling Tessa.

"Let's do this thing," I say excitedly, wrapping my arms around his waist and walking into the family room with the loves of my life.

Chapter Eleven

Jacob

The sun barely kisses the sky when I start the ascent into reality from my dreamworld. A soft pair of lips wrap around my cock and suck me into a hot, wet mouth. I come fully awake with a start and fist my hands in the sheet at my sides. Holy shit! This is turning out to be the best Christmas ever.

"Don't stop," I say gruffly as her hand joins her mouth to work my shaft perfectly.

Kara hums her acknowledgment around my dick, and I feel my balls begin to tighten.

"Do you have any idea how gorgeous you are when you do that?" I grit out, trying to hold off on coming down her throat. My hands gently pull her hair away from her face, so I can get a better view of her blowing my mind, pun intended.

I try to force my brain to remember that it's Christmas morning and that the girls could be down here at any minute to wake us up, but her mouth feels so damn good that I can't find the necessary restraint. Instead, I grab Kara under her armpits and haul her up the bed and onto her back. I roll on top of her and put my hand between her legs.

Thank God we fell asleep naked. My need for her is palpable. You'd think it's been weeks not hours since the last time I had her.

"Please be ready," I whisper just as my fingers find her hot, wet and ready to take me.

I replace my hand with my cock and thrust into her to the hilt. Kara's head flies back, and her mouth opens on a silent moan.

"Quick and rough, Kara. We don't have a lot of time," I grunt out as I start moving in her.

"Yes. God, yes!" Her arms wrap around my shoulder and pulls me down for a deep kiss.

There is nothing better than waking up to Kara's face, especially when she's caught up in the pleasure that only I can give her. If I could take a picture of how fucking sexy she looks right now and keep it with me all the time, I surely would.

"You feel so good, Jacob!" Kara cries out. Her tight little cunt starts fluttering with her impending release.

Knowing I finally found my other half and that tomorrow she's choosing to love me for the rest of her life is the most wonderful feeling I've ever known. There aren't words to describe what it feels like when that missing puzzle piece clicks into place, making your life complete. I waited a long time to feel this content. I even thought I had it once before, but I was sorely mistaken. Now my heart is bursting with happiness and love.

Speaking of bursting…

"Fuck!" I shout when my orgasm slams into me unexpectedly. Kara moans underneath me as she climaxes as well.

Staying connected to her, I pull the covers up over us in case the girls come downstairs. I wouldn't want to scar them for life by giving them an eye full.

"Merry Christmas," Kara whispers and peppers my face with kisses.

"Merry Christmas, Sunshine." I slowly pull out of her, enjoying the feel of every inch of her and collapse on my back.

"We need to put some clothes on," Kara says, yet makes no move towards dressing.

I roll her towards me and slap her ass. You can hear the crack of skin on skin echoing into the silence.

"Ow! That hurt!" She reaches around and rubs her butt.

Whoops! Maybe it was a little harder than I expected.

"Want me to kiss it and make it better?" I reach around to do just that.

"You are incorrigible! Don't touch my ass!" She pushes me away and scrambles off the bed. "Now, get dressed!"

"Yes ma'am!" I love it when she goes all no nonsense on me.

We dress in sweats and t-shirts and then head upstairs before we can get trampled by a couple of miniature sumo wrestlers.

The house is eerily quiet as Kara and I enter the kitchen. Emma sits at the table sipping a cup of coffee, no doubt enjoying the peace while she can get it. I grab a mug from the cupboard and fill it to the brim, needing some caffeine after the little sleep I got. Kara fills her own and squeezes my arm before going into the living room in order to give me some alone time with Emma.

"Merry Christmas," I murmur and kiss her head.

"Merry Christmas," Emma says in a low voice and barely musters up a smile for me.

I sit in the chair next to her and sip my coffee, carefully watching her. There are worry lines that weren't present last time I was here and without makeup, you can see the dark circles under her eyes.

"Want to talk about it?" I ask, hoping that nothing is seriously wrong. I couldn't imagine what I would do if anything was wrong with my sister. It feels like a punch to the gut imagining all the things that could possibly be wrong. A tingling ball of anxiety presses in on my chest at the thought of anything bad happening to her. She's my rock, and my biggest confidante since my mom died.

She lets out a long sigh, but doesn't say anything.

I grab her hand and squeeze lightly. "Sis, you need to tell me what's going on. It's obvious that you're run down and tired. You aren't sick are you?"

I hate vocalizing that concern for fear that it will be true because I was stupid enough to do so. I stop myself just shy of knocking on the wood table for luck.

"I'm just tired, Jacob. My life is contained within the four walls of this house. I'm a wife and a mother. The girls are getting older and are more of a handful. They fight more. They whine more. They want to do more activities. And I'm doing it all alone. John works eighty hours a week. He travels at least twenty out of the fifty-two weeks a year. I'm just tired. Of everything."

I watch as tears stain her lovely cheeks and I fist my hands, fighting the urge to pummel my brother-in-law for being oblivious to the strain my sister is under.

"Have you tried talking to him?"

She lets out a humorless laugh. "Of course I have. He's just as tired as I am, but for an entirely different reason. One thing I know for sure is that life is often unfair and it will repeatedly kick your ass."

She sounds so dejected and helpless. This isn't my sister. And I'm disheartened by it.

"Hey," I squeeze her hand again to get her attention. "Don't say that. Didn't you once tell me that you have to fight for what matters? Well fight for your family, Emma. Make John open his eyes before it's too late. You two need to work this out, not just for you but for those girls too."

A sigh and a short nod is the only answer she gives me. It pains me to see my sister hurting so deeply.

I'm beginning to think my thoughts about being closer to family aren't too far off the mark. Between Kara wanting to have a baby and Emma needing help with the girls, it makes sense. I wonder how Kara would feel about leaving the city.

"I'm surprised the girls aren't up yet." Changing the subject seems like the best thing to do. I look at the clock to see it is going on six-thirty. This is late for them.

"I give it another ten minutes or so before they come barreling out here. Enjoy it while you can, baby brother." Emma finally gives me a real smile, and it confirms that changing the subject was the best move.

"Brad and Sophie had their baby early this morning." I push my phone across the table and watch as she takes in the sight of the beautiful baby picture that Brad sent me.

"What did they name him?"

"Duncan Jacob. Crazy, right?" I chuckle at the thought of them naming him after me. It's the highest honor they could have given me.

"That's sweet." Emma takes another sip of her coffee and sits back in her chair. "I can't believe Brad has a baby... Hell, I can't believe you're getting married tomorrow. It's not exactly the way I pictured it, but I think it's perfect for you two. Oh, before I forget, Dad will be in town later this morning. He'll be here for the wedding."

"Good. I was worried he'd have to work. It wouldn't feel right without him here."

"Agreed."

"Kara and I decided to try for kids sooner rather than later." I'm usually not one to spill my guts, but I have a feeling my sister needs this right now.

Just as I anticipated, her face lights up and she looks years younger than she did a few minutes ago.

"That is so wonderful!" She claps her hands and exclaims. "I cannot wait to be an aunt. I'm going to spoil your children rotten and make you regret the years of torment you put me through with the girls."

I feign horror. "You wouldn't, horse breath!"

"Oh, I so would, penis face!"

Kara joins us in the kitchen when she hears us laughing.

"My parents just woke up. And I saw John heading into Grace's room." She sits on my lap and wraps her arms around my neck. Leaning over I kiss the tip of her nose.

At the sound of little girl voices and high pitched squeals, Emma stands up. "And that would be my cue to get their stockings out."

"Is everything okay?" Kara asks when Emma leaves the room.

"It will be. I hope…" My voice trails off as I look out the doorway into the living room. I'll wait until after the wedding to bring up moving. Kara doesn't need to be concerned with that just yet. Besides it will give me a chance to work on my case. They say the best defense is a strong offense.

"What do you say, Sunshine? Want to go open some presents?"

"I'd love to." She leans in and rubs her nose alongside mine before planting a quick kiss to my lips.

"Let the fun begin," I shout as we join everyone in the living room.

"And this one's for you," Kara says as she hands me my present. I'm immediately surprised by how heavy it is for its size.

I grab her hand before she can walk away, and I press the jewelry box in her hand. "You forgot one."

I smirk as she excitedly bounces into her seat. Watching her get presents never gets old. Every reaction from Kara is a genuine one. She's never fake, and I appreciate the hell out of it.

The living room is covered in torn wrapping paper and shredded bows. The girls are playing in the corner with their new iPad minis, while the grown ups open the last of the gifts.

Today has been one of the best Christmas' I can remember in a long time. The girls both have on the matching Christmas pajamas that they got, that they'll spend the day in. Emma and I used to love getting to stay in our pajamas all day. I'm glad she continued with that tradition.

Maggie is in the kitchen making everyone breakfast. A huge feast, including breakfast burritos, is Kara's family tradition on Christmas morning. She vows that breakfast will be delicious, and that I'm going to crave these burritos every year hereafter. I swear the Andrews women are trying to give me a gut. I'll just have to keep finding creative ways with my girl to burn off the extra calories.

Bill and Maggie were gracious enough to gift us with a honeymoon for Christmas. Because the money they have saved for Kara's wedding wasn't needed, they thought it would be good to use it for the honeymoon. It was more than we could have ever asked for and extremely thoughtful of them. The more I think about it, the more anxious I am to whisk my girl away for two weeks of uninterrupted sexy time.

Surprisingly enough, the munchkins haven't realized that they didn't get a gift from Kara and me. Bill is sneaking next door to get the puppies as we speak. I've been assured by Kara that they will have a green ribbon and a red ribbon tied around their respective necks. Luckily, we were able to get the brother, sister pair from the picture Emma had sent us.

Emma still doesn't know we got two dogs, and I'm starting to feel guilty after our conversation earlier. She certainly doesn't need any additional stress.

Before we leave, I'll lecture the girls on responsibility and will make them promise that they'll take care of them without complaint, or I'll have to take them back. Scaring them into submission works most of the time.

I make quick work of the wrapping paper on my gift and open the box to find a new handgun. I pick it up and study the Kimber .45 pistol. Wow... this is quite a gun.

"Holy cow! How'd you know to pick this out?" I gush and turn my attention to Kara, who is fiddling with the bow on her unopened gift.

"Mack went with me. You like it?"

"Like it? I love it! Thank you!" I lean over and kiss her thoroughly. Emma and John's catcalls make me pull away.

"Thank you," I whisper against her mouth.

Gesturing to her gift, I tell her to hurry up. I'm dying for her to see the necklace.

She gives me a mischievous grin and rips open the package. She opens the velvet box and reveals a silver necklace with a large round yellow diamond surrounded by tiny white diamonds. She picks up the card that I tucked into the velvet, and I watch her hands tremble as she opens and reads it.

Thank you for shining your light on me and warming my heart when I thought it was permanently frozen. I love you from the bottom of my soul and will spend the rest of my life giving back to you all that you give to me.

I watch as her chin quivers and tears pour out of her eyes. "Happy tears! I promise!" She gives me a watery smile and a little sputtering laugh.

"Put it on me!" She exclaims and lifts her hair so that I can latch it around her neck.

I run my finger down her neck and over her chest, before fingering the diamond. The gem sits on her like it was meant to be there. Perfect.

"I love it! Thank you! Thank you! Thank you!" She says in between kisses.

"Anything for you, Sunshine." And I mean that more today than yesterday. Every day with her gets better and better.

A few minutes later I hear the door to the mudroom open.

Cue our rehearsed spiel.

"Hey, Kara. Did you forget to pack the gifts for the girls?" I say loud enough for them to hear me across the room.

Their fingers stop moving and their heads shoot up to stare us down.

"Hmmm… I'm not sure. I thought I brought them, but I definitely didn't see them under the tree. I wonder if Santa took them back when he came last night," she says innocently, playing along perfectly.

"Were you girls bad? Is that why Santa took your presents with him?" I ask with a serious tone to my voice.

They both shake their head in unison with a dire look on their faces.

"Then they have to be around here somewhere," I exclaim and stand up. "Maybe you should help me find them."

Bill walks out into the living room and winks to let me know that we are all set. Perfect timing.

The girls get up and start looking under chairs and behind cushions. It's comical really. The longer it takes to locate the present, the more frantic their searching becomes.

"Maybe I left them in the mudroom?" I murmur and both the girls take off in that direction.

When the door to the mudroom opens, the house is filled with yips and squeals of delight as the girls and the puppies get to know one another.

"A puppy!" Grace shrieks and runs at warp speed into the living room with the girl puppy held tightly in her arms. The puppy licks her face enthusiastically.

"Two puppies!" Candace follows suit running in after her sister with the boy puppy.

"Two puppies?" Emma turns and gives me the stink eye. I give her a sheepish look in return and shrug my shoulders. Then for good measure, I point to Kara behind her back trying to blame the whole thing on her.

All I get in return is a "Yeah right" look and a shake of her fist. I'll have to make sure I'm never alone with her from now until the time we leave. Otherwise, she might kick me in the balls.

"What are you guys going to name them?" Kara asks from her spot on the floor where she's playing with the dogs.

"I want to name my Simba," Candace announces. "He looks like a Simba."

"If he's Simba, then mine can be Nala!" Grace shouts excitedly.

"Your sister is going to kill you," John whispers as he comes to stand next to me.

"You should talk," I scoff under my breath and then realize what I've done.

"What is that supposed to mean?" He asks sounding offended.

"Dude, I'm not going to get involved, but you need to talk to your wife. She's run down and tired. If you don't open your eyes, you just might lose the best thing that's ever happened to you – your family." I take a sip of my coffee and look at him out of the corner of my eye. A muscle in his jaw ticks and his fists clench. I refuse to apologize for overstepping my bounds and looking out for Emma's best interest. It's what a good brother should do.

"The only thing stopping me from decking you right now is that I know you're coming from a good place. In the future, keep your fucking mouth shut."

My mouth gapes as I watch John storm away. I've never seen him so pissed off. Emma gives me a glare and a worried look after witnessing his departure.

Shit.

I scrub my hands down my face and hope like hell I didn't just make things worse.

Lying on the floor of the basement with two puppies crawling over me, I smile when Kara lies down next to me. I reach over and lace my fingers with hers.

I promised the girls I would watch their dogs while they went to their grandparents' house for a few hours. They weren't too keen on leaving, but I finally convinced them that they would be just fine while they were gone.

Thankfully, Kara's parents decided to go to the movies tonight after my sister and her brood left. Alone time with my girl is just how I want to end my Christmas.

"Did you have a good Christmas, Sunshine?" I bring her hand up to my lips and kiss each of her fingertips.

"Mmm… I did. It was the best one yet." She rolls on her side to face me. "I love you. So damn much."

I pick Nala up, who has now weaseled her way in between us and set her off to the side so I can grab Kara and pull her closer.

"I love you too, babe." I tuck her head under my chin and lightly stroke her back.

"I can't wait to marry you tomorrow," she whispers before planting a soft kiss on my chest.

"Me too." I kiss her hair and rest my cheek on her head. "Me too."

"Um, Jacob?" Kara starts to squirm, but I refuse to let her go.

"Jacob," she says more forcefully this time.

"What?" I ask, slightly annoyed that she's ruining our quiet moment together.

"One of the dogs just tinkled on my leg." Her voice sounds horrified.

I throw my head back and roar with laughter. Thank God they pissed on her and not me. I don't care if that makes me a son of a bitch or not.

Kara jumps up and starts to squirm out of her pants, cursing and muttering under her breath.

I sit up and grab her arm, pulling her down to me once her pants are off. I roll her under me and kiss her breathlessly.

"There's still time to make some more Christmas memories." My lips suck on her neck where it meets her shoulder and a low moan leaves her mouth.

"I'd like that," she whispers.

Spending the next two hours inside my girl – my future – is the perfect ending, to the perfect holiday. And tomorrow, the rest of our lives begin.

Chapter Twelve

Sam

There is wrapping paper everywhere. And I do mean *everywhere*. I think Tessa thought it was more fun to throw paper around then it was to actually have new toys to play with.

It's the little things that mean so much.

I really wanted this Christmas to be special for her. Especially since this is going to be the last one with just her.

"VIP tickets for the Dave Matthews concert in D.C. next April! That's pretty awesome. Thanks, honey," Aiden says after opening what he thinks is his last gift.

Tessa is sitting next to us on the floor playing with her Big Hugs Elmo, oblivious to everything but her toy. I feel like shouting, "Take that Aiden!"

I knew that toy would be a hit! I just hope that woman found another one. I still feel a touch guilty about that.

"It's your turn," Aiden murmurs as he reaches under the couch for a gorgeously wrapped box. It's the unmistakable size for jewelry, and my heart picks up. I love when he gets me jewelry. There is always something thoughtful and meaningful behind his purchases.

I reach out and snatch the box from his hand, bouncing up and down while I rip off the bow and unwrap the shiny red and silver paper. The rectangular, blue velvet box creaks as I open it. I gasp as I take in the exquisite charm bracelet. It's platinum and dainty, made up of multiple infinity knots linked together with charms hanging from them. I finger the charms as Aiden goes through each one. "The 'B' is for your Red Sox, the book is for your writing, the aquamarine heart is for Tessa, and the dog is for Hugo. Then there is your birthstone and mine. And this heart… is because you are the keeper of mine."

"It's… I don't know what to say." I look up at him with blurry, tear filled eyes. "It's perfect. Thank you." I smile and hold out my wrist for him to put it on me. I move my arm back and forth, looking at each charm as it shifts.

I settle into Aiden's side. His arm rests around my shoulders, holding me tightly to his body while we watch our daughter play. Everything about this moment is perfect. I couldn't ask for anything more in life. I'm fulfilled in ways I could never have imagined before.

"Well, as much as I would love to lay here all day with you in my arms watching our angel play, I better go get in the shower. Then we need to get her dressed so we can go to my mothers." Aiden moves to get up, and I launch myself at him.

"Not yet. I think Santa left a gift over there." I point to the corner of the room, where a large package sits propped against the wall, hidden behind a rocking chair. It's wrapped in white and red striped paper with a big bow on it.

"What is that?" He asks before getting up and looking at the tag on the gift. "To Aiden. Love, Santa."

He lifts his gaze to me and quirks his eyebrow playfully. "Love, Santa?"

I laugh at his facial expression. "Is there something I should know about you and Santa?" I joke with him.

"Mrs. Claus and me, sure. Santa and Me." He shakes his head and gives me a grim look. "Not so much."

"Aren't you going to open it?" I start squirming like an anxious child, waiting for him to open his last gift.

He doesn't keep me waiting long. After he brings the gift back to the couch, he rips off the paper and opens the white box, revealing a bunch of white tissue paper. I bite my lip in anticipation as he moves the paper aside.

Nestled in the paper is a three foot canvas portrait of Tessa standing in a winter wonderland. She's dressed in a white, silk dress with a red velvet sash and bow. There are red roses around the bottom of the dress, and the tulle petticoat gives it extra flounce. Her legs are encased in white tights with a rose floral design, and her feet are donning a pair of metallic gold ballet flats, embellished with a bow at the toe. Holding her silky, blonde curls back is a red headband with a red silk bow. Her smile lights up the whole canvas. She is such a happy child.

My throat clogs at how fucking adorable my little girl is. I'm so lucky God blessed me with her.

"This picture is gorgeous," Aiden breathes. His finger lovingly grazes over the image of our daughter.

"It is, isn't it? Look at the next one." I can't wait to hang that picture over the fireplace, but it's the next one that has my heart racing.

He gently sets the canvas aside and digs through the paper once more. He pulls out a framed eight inch by ten inch picture of Tessa sitting on a wooden stool against a simple white background. She has a big smile on her face, and her little index fingers are pointing to her white shirt with pink and green letters, that says "I'm gonna be a Big Sister".

Aiden looks up at me with a look of astonishment. "Is this true? Are you having my baby again?" He asks.

I nod and give him a watery smile. We've been trying for six months now to get pregnant again. As soon as I missed my period, I raced to the drug store to buy a pregnancy test. I felt bad not telling him right away, but with Christmas around the corner, I wanted it to be special.

He reaches out and places his hand on my still flat stomach. "Best Christmas present ever," he whispers before leaning down and kissing my belly where his hand had laid.

I barely suppress the sob that rips from my chest as happy tears flow down my face. I never knew it was possible to be this happy.

The doorbell ringing has me racing the rest of the way down the stairs with Tessa in my arms. She clings to my neck and laughs a loud, belly laugh as I bounce her up and down.

"Will you please be careful?" Aiden reprimands me from his place on the couch in the family room.

I roll my eyes and huff. It's going to be a long eight months with him breathing down my neck. Luckily, it comes from a good place otherwise I'd have to kill him.

I open the door and am greeted by the sight of Michelle and Kyle. Taking in their appearance, I immediately laugh at poor Kyle. His arms are overloaded with presents, so much so that I can barely see his face.

"He's my elf for the day," Michelle smiles and mutters by way of explanation, before grabbing my daughter from me.

"Aunt Shelly is here to spoil my goddaughter rotten!" She exclaims and makes her way into the family room. She kisses Aiden on the cheek and sets Tessa down by the tree.

"Let me look at you!" Michelle coos at Tessa, holding her arms out. "Oh my God! This just might be the cutest little outfit I've ever seen!"

I have to agree with that assessment. Tessa looks like a miniature Mrs. Claus. Well… if Mrs. Claus was chic and fashionable. She's dressed in a red, cable sweater dress with fur collar and cuffs. There are white snowflakes down the front and white hearts along the hem. Her golden curls flow from underneath a red and white snowflake beret with a fur pompom. And her white tights have reindeer and hearts up the side. She really is to die for in that outfit.

I might have a tad bit of an addiction to dressing my daughter. Sue me. It's just too much fun.

"She is quite a doll," Kyle replies, as he strategically rids himself of all the boxes and bags he was toting. I have to give the guy credit, he did that like an expert. If they gave out Olympic medals for that event, Kyle would be the World Champion for sure.

"What the hell?" Michelle screeches. My eyes dart over to where she is kneeling in front of the coffee table with Tessa at her side. Her eyes are fixated on the picture I gave to Aiden for his office. When she finally looks up at me for an answer, I see tears streaming down her face. I smile back and nod my head.

"My best friend is having another baby?" She screams. Then she sniffles and jumps up to give me a tight, loving embrace. I latch onto her, knowing exactly how she feels. It's the same way I felt when I found out she was getting married. The love I have for her is like the love I would have for a sister. It knows no bounds.

"I'm so happy for you," she whispers in my ear as she rocks our bodies back and forth.

"Thank you," I whisper back. I give her a tight squeeze and then pull away.

"Enough of the water works ladies. We need to get a move on or we are going to be late for the festivities at my mothers," Aiden chides us affectionately.

"Yeah, yeah. Whatever." Michelle sniffles and waves him off.

I spend the next hour watching Tessa and Michelle playing with toys and showing off new clothes like Vanna White, while Kyle and Aiden huddle off to the side discussing football. Christmas isn't all about giving and receiving gifts. That's just an added bonus – being able to show people how much we care and that we are thinking of them. The real beauty of Christmas is spending time with the ones you love and knowing that no matter what, you'll always have each other.

"Wake up, honey." Aiden's gentle voice penetrates my sleep. My upper body gently sways when his hands give me a little shake.

"Mmmm," is all I can muster up as slumber starts to pull me under once again. I vaguely hear his chuckle, but I can't respond.

A few minutes later, I feel cold air hit my face, sending goosebumps down my neck. A light shines and starts to penetrate the shield of my eyelids. I grumble in the back of my throat and try to burrow into my coat.

"Rise and shine," Aiden mumbles in my ear.

I slowly open my eyes and begrudgingly blink the sleep away. I absolutely adore sleeping in the car. Add to that the fact that I'm pregnant and didn't get much sleep last night, and I'm surprised he was even able to wake me up.

Today was a long, boisterous day. My mother-in-law's house was full to the brim with aunts, cousins, siblings and children.

The only quiet reprieve I got today was when Aiden followed me to the bathroom and surprised me by bending me over the vanity for a quickie. That was hot and fun all right. My face splits into a knowing grin as Aiden pulls me out of the car by my hand.

"What's that look for?" He asks and kisses my nose. His arms draw me closer and his scent envelopes me.

"Just remembering our love making session in the bath-room today." I can feel the heat blanketing my body as the memories wash over me.

"Let's get Tessa to bed and we can have another ses-sion, but in our room this time. I'll be sure to take my time with you and drive you crazy during this round." His fingers trace the seam of my jeans between my legs, and I instinc-tively move closer to his body, wanting more.

"Am I going to get to play this time? I want to suck you hard and deep…" My voice trails off and Aiden makes a pained noise.

"You're such a tease. Let's go. I'll get Tessa and carry her to bed." Aiden steps away from me and opens the back door to the truck in order to retrieve a sleeping Tessa from her car seat. My body is still humming, and I instantly miss his warmth.

"Lily and Michael were cute today. I really hope that something progresses there. I think he'd be good for her and draw her out of her shell. Maybe make her a little more social," I chatter as we make our way into the house. Lily seems to have connected with Aiden's second cousin, and I couldn't be more thrilled for her.

"Yeah, we'll see. Try not to meddle too much. I'm sure it will work out just fine if you leave them alone," he responds after dumping his coat onto the couch.

"Who me?" I ask, slightly offended that he thinks I would meddle.

The only response I get is a quirk of his eyebrow before he heads for the stairs.

I follow him upstairs and watch as he takes Tessa's coat and dress off. He gently pulls a nightgown over her head and sticks her arms through, before laying her down and covering her with the blankets. I'll never tire of watching the two of them together. It amazes me how soft and tender this big, virile, masculine man can be.

I move to the side of the crib and kiss my fingertips before pressing them to her partially open mouth. My hand drags down her body and pats her diapered bottom.

Aiden takes my hand and leads me to the bedroom, where we waste no time stripping each other bare and exploring every part of each other. And once we're sweaty, panting and completely spent, we fall asleep wrapped in each other's arms.

This was by far the best, merry little Christmas I've ever had. And I know they're just going to get better.

Merry Christmas to all! And to all a good night!

About the Author

Jessica is the author of the Love Square series. She grew up in Central New York, where she spends her days as a Security Analyst at an IT consulting company. In her free time, she enjoys reading books and developing ideas for her own stories. Writing is her secret passion that she's been fostering since elementary school, when she wrote her first book about a puppy. It has always been a dream of hers to be able to share her stories with the world.

Jessica currently lives in New York with her husband and three dogs.

Visit my website at:
www.jessicaingro.com

Other Books by Jessica:
Love Square (Love Square #1)
His Ever After (Love Square #2)

4959336R00081

Printed in Great Britain
by Amazon.co.uk, Ltd.,
Marston Gate.